THE WITCHES OF FAIRHOLLOW HIGH

The NEW Girl

ARIANA CHAMBERS

EGMONT

With special thanks to
Siobhan Curham and Catherine Coe

EGMONT

We bring stories to life

First published in Great Britain 2016
by Egmont UK Limited
The Yellow Building, 1 Nicholas Road, London W11 4AN

Copyright © Egmont UK Ltd, 2016

ISBN 978 1 4052 7740 2

www.egmont.co.uk

A CIP catalogue record for this title is available from the British Library

Typeset by Avon DataSet Ltd, Bidford on Avon, Warwickshire
Printed and bound in Great Britain by the CPI Group

59670/1

One of my favourite feel-good film scenes of all time is from a movie called *Winter Vacation*. In it, the main character, Lola, has just arrived home from college for Christmas. She's trudging through the airport feeling all gloomy because she thinks her boyfriend, Josh, is going to be away for the holidays visiting his dad. But as she walks into Arrivals she sees Josh waiting for her with a big soppy grin on his face. He's holding one of those little cardboard signs with her name on it and *I love you, Peanut!* written underneath ('Peanut' is his nickname for her, but that's a whole other story). The second Lola sees him, she flings herself over the barrier and into his arms. Every time my best friend Ellie and I watch that scene – even after about five hundred viewings – we tear up. Every time, without fail.

As I walk into the Arrivals hall of Newbridge Airport, trying to keep my trolley wheels straight and my guitar from sliding off my tower of cases, I can't help scanning the line of people at the barrier hopefully. Even though I know Aunt Clara isn't able to meet me because she has to be at her shop for a delivery, and even though there's absolutely no one else to come and meet me, because:

a) I don't have a boyfriend like Josh,

b) I don't have a boyfriend, period,

c) I don't know anyone other than Aunt Clara in this place, my eyes still search for a piece of cardboard with my name. But there's only one person holding a sign, a chubby man with a red face, wearing a too-tight suit. His sign says *MR BAILEY*. Definitely not Nessa Reid. Definitely not me. I sigh and push my trolley past the line of people, trying to look all cool and nonchalant, like I don't care that I've been sent to this stupid place, in the middle of nowhere, with *no friends* and no one to even come and meet me at the airport. As my guitar almost slides off the trolley again I think of my dad and feel a stab of anger. He gave me the guitar as a going-away gift – like that's going to make up for the fact that he deserted me to go and work in Dubai, in the Middle East. At least I have something I can write angry songs about bad parents on, I guess.

I look around the Arrivals hall. Dad told me that the taxi rank would be on my right. I didn't realise that he'd meant literally. The airport is so tiny I can actually see the taxis lined up on the other side of the glass wall. I push my trolley over to the doors. As they slide apart I'm hit by a sharp blast of cold air. When I left London the weather was bright and sunny, but here in Scotland the December sky is a dull, heavy white, like a thick layer of cotton wool. My trolley clatters on the paving stones as I walk over to the first cab in the line. I fumble in my pocket for the piece of paper Dad gave me with Aunt Clara's address on it, even though I've studied it so many times during the flight that I know it by heart. I've got a horrible anxious feeling in my stomach.

'Please can you take me to Paper Soul on Fairhollow High Street?' I say to the driver as he gets out of his taxi and opens the boot. He has short silver-grey hair and a slightly flattened nose, like he might have broken it once in a fight.

'Paper what?' he says, picking up one of my cases.

'Paper Soul. It's a bookshop – and café.' This is the one good thing about being sent to stay with Aunt Clara – I'll be living above a café and a bookshop, two of my favourite things in one building. 'It's next to the chemist's,' I add, looking back at Dad's directions.

'Ah,' the driver says knowingly. 'That place.'

He doesn't exactly sound impressed. I get into the back of the cab and try not to wonder why. As

I stuff the piece of paper back into my pocket my fingers brush against my mum's locket. Instantly, I feel better.

My mum passed away when I was very young – not long after I had been sick in hospital myself as a baby. I don't really remember her, and Dad doesn't talk about her very much, but last night when I was packing to leave he gave me this locket. 'It was hers, and she would have wanted you to have it,' he said gruffly. It's beautiful, small and silver with a five-pointed star delicately engraved on the front, and I love the way it feels in my hand.

As the driver pulls away from the airport, I close my eyes and play the *Worse Off Than You* game. This is a game I invented during a particularly grim Science test involving the Periodic Table. The idea is that whenever you're feeling really stressed about something, you just have to think of a much worse scenario and it will instantly make your own problem feel smaller. I imagine a girl my age, thirteen, stranded in the middle of the

Sahara Desert. She hasn't had anything to drink for days and a herd of snorting camels are about to stampede her. I open my eyes and look out of the window. We're driving along a narrow country lane, surrounded by bare, stubbly fields. It looks pretty bleak, but at least there are no stampeding camels and I have a bottle of water in my bag. I take it out and have a sip. There really are a lot of people a lot worse off than me. This really isn't the end of the world . . . it just feels like it.

Eventually, we leave the twisty turny lanes and pull on to a slightly wider road. We're still surrounded by fields, but every so often a car passes us so I guess we must be getting closer to Fairhollow. I press my face up against the cold window. The sky is now darkening from white to grey, as if someone's shading it in with a pencil. I feel a flutter of anxiety in the pit of my stomach. I haven't seen Aunt Clara since she last came to visit me and Dad, when I was about six. I wonder if she's changed much. I have a memory of her from that day, filed away in my head like an old photo. She's standing in the back garden, staring blankly ahead, her long golden hair blowing in the wind. I think she and Dad had just had an argument. I can remember Dad marching into the house and the back door slamming. I also remember Aunt Clara hugging me when she was leaving. She smelt like rose petals. I start to relax a bit. Hopefully it will be nice living with Mum's sister – and hopefully I can find out more about Mum.

The road starts curving up a really steep hill.

'Soon be there,' the driver says, looking at me in the rear-view mirror.

I nod back at him. 'Thank you.'

Finally, we reach the top of the hill and there's something other than fields to look at. A town is spread out far below us, in the base of a huge valley, surrounded on either side by thick ridges of woodland.

'You from Fairhollow?' the driver asks as the road starts cutting down through the trees.

I shake my head. 'No. My mum is – was. I'm going to stay with my aunt.'

'Interesting place,' the driver says. But again, something about the way he says it doesn't make it sound like a good thing.

'What do you mean?'

'You'll see.' As our eyes meet in the rear-view mirror, the anxious feeling returns to the pit of my stomach. I look out of the window. The tree branches are spread above us like a canopy and pale wintery light is filtering through them. It would have looked really pretty if the sun was shining. Finally, we emerge from the woods and I see a sign by the road saying *WELCOME TO FAIRHOLLOW*. Someone has scrawled something underneath in red but it's too small for me to make out what.

The road we're on leads directly to Fairhollow High Street. We go past a row of tall grand houses. They all look a bit faded and worn, though, with peeling paintwork and grimy windows. When the driver stops at a crossroads and a group of kids about my age cross in front of us my skin prickles with fear. Tomorrow, I'll be joining my new school. I think of my best friend, Ellie, again and I feel a pang of sorrow. Ellie and I have gone to school together for what feels like forever. I can't imagine lessons without her. It feels all wrong. I watch the kids as they head into a café called The Cup and Saucer. They're all laughing and joking, deep in conversation. The traffic light turns green and the driver heads on down the High Street. It all looks really olde worlde and there's no sign of any kind of supermarket. Then I spot Paper Soul at the very end of the road. It's a tall thin building, three storeys high. Its sign is hand-painted, red lettering on a black background with a silver crescent moon in the corner. As the driver pulls up, I see a dimly-lit display of books in the window.

'All right, love?' The driver looks over his shoulder at me.

I nod. But I feel anything but as I follow him out of the taxi. My head is stuffed full of *what if*s.

What if Aunt Clara and I don't get along? What if she doesn't really want me here? What if I hate it here? What if I don't make any new friends?

The driver brings me my cases and I pay him with some of the money Dad gave me this morning.

I wait until he's driven off and then I open the door to the shop. A bell above me jangles loudly, making me jump.

'Hello,' I say, nervously, as I step inside.

The shop smells of a weird mixture of incense and baking bread. As my eyes adjust to the darkness, I see tall alcoves lined with books on either side of me. Just in front of me, there's a stand-alone display. I do a quick scan of the titles: *Ghost Hunting for Dummies, Haunted Castles, Spirits and Spectres*. I frown. Why would Aunt Clara have a display of books like that? My dad's always said that supernatural stuff should be renamed *super-stupid*. He reckons that people only go on about ghosts and stuff nowadays to keep trick-or-treaters in sweets. Maybe Aunt Clara got the books in for some kind of Halloween promotion and hasn't bothered taking them down yet. I scan the shop for a teen fiction section. But everywhere I look seems to be the same kind of stuff: *Astrology, Spirituality, New Age, Healing.* I feel a pang of disappointment. In my mind, I'd been picturing Aunt Clara's shop as cosy and bright, filled with other teenagers chatting about books, but this is more like a really old library. Hopefully the café part will be a bit more cheerful.

I drag my cases past two more alcoves of books and the shop opens out into the café area. It's completely deserted. There's a counter running along the back, with a handful of round tables arranged in front of it. At the centre of each table there are thick, red candles with trails of wax run down their sides like bulging veins.

'Aunt Clara!' I call, really loud now. This place is starting to give me the creeps.

I hear a door slamming out back and the sound of footsteps. Then Aunt Clara appears in the doorway behind the counter. At least, I think it must be Aunt Clara – she looks totally different to how I remember her. Her long hair has been cut into a sharp bob that just skims her shoulders and it's been dyed flame red. She's wearing a long black dress, and the only splash of colour on her – apart from her hair – is the bright turquoise pendant she's wearing on a long silver chain around her neck. She looks at me and gasps.

'I'm Nessa,' I say. My face instantly starts to burn. I have this really annoying habit of flushing bright red any time I'm nervous.

'Yes, I know,' Aunt Clara says, still staring at me. 'You look so . . .'

She comes out from behind the counter and stands right in front of me. Her icy blue eyes are ringed with black eyeliner, making them look even more striking. She reaches out and takes hold of a lock of my hair. It probably is too long – it's almost down to my elbows now. I know from the one photo Dad gave me that I look like my mum. I get the same anxious bubbling in my stomach that I got in the cab, but way stronger this time, so strong it's making my legs go weak.

'You look so much like Celeste,' Aunt Clara whispers. But she doesn't smile.

'Can I – is it OK if I sit down?' I gesture at one of the tables.

'Of course. Yes. Do. You must be tired. And hungry. Are you hungry? I'll get you something to eat.' Aunt Clara seems really nervous too, and it makes me realise what a big deal this must be for her. She never got married or had any children, and now she's been lumbered with a thirteen-year-old she barely knows – one who looks exactly like her dead sister.

Even though I'm not hungry, I nod, not wanting to upset her. She hurries off behind the counter and returns with a glass of really bright orange juice and a chocolate brownie. I smile in relief. If there's one thing guaranteed to make me feel better it's a chocolate brownie. I take a huge bite. Ugh! It takes all of my willpower not to spit it straight out again. It tastes vile.

'Ah, you're obviously not used to beetroot brownies,' Aunt Clara says.

I stare up at her. 'Beetroot?' *Who puts beetroot in a brownie?!*

'Yes. It's a vegan recipe. This is a vegan café,' Aunt Clara explains, pointing to a blackboard on the wall with *Soup of the Day: Pumpkin Seed and Potato* written on it in chalk.

I manage to swallow the mouthful of brownie without retching and reach for my orange juice to help get rid of the taste. But that's even more disgusting.

'It's carrot juice,' Aunt Clara says.

'It's lovely,' I lie.

Aunt Clara raises her eyebrows. 'Don't worry, lots of people hate vegan food at first but you'll soon get used to it.'

I frown. She's caught me out.

Aunt Clara shifts awkwardly from one foot to the other. She has silver rings on every one of her fingers, including her thumbs. My eyes are drawn to one on her little finger, a cat's head with emerald eyes. 'Once you get used to organic, sugar-free foods, you'll never want to eat anything else,' she says. 'It's so full of flavour.'

I take another bite of my beetroot brownie and force myself to swallow. Aunt Clara looks down at me like she might be about to say something but she stays silent. I smile at her. It makes my face ache.

One thing's for sure, if I'm going to stay here without hurting Aunt Clara's feelings, I'm going to have to work a whole lot harder on my lying skills.

I once read in a magazine that the very first thought you have the moment you wake up is the most important thought you will have all day. Apparently your first thought sets the tone for the rest of the day, so you should try your hardest to make it a happy one.

The very first thought I have the moment I wake up the following morning is *Oh no*! Swiftly followed by *I'm still in Fairhollow and I have to go to school!* I really hope that magazine article was wrong, otherwise today is totally doomed.

I turn on my bedside lamp and grab my phone. I have two new text messages, one from Dad and one from Ellie. I read Ellie's first as I'm still officially upset with Dad.

How did you sleep? Xxx

I quickly type a reply.

Not good. My stomach kept making really weird noises. I'm not sure if it was hunger or fear xoxo

Last night's dinner was something called quinoa. It was like eating soggy seeds, even worse than the beetroot brownie. I ended up telling Aunt Clara I was too tired to eat very much and going to bed at eight o'clock. I didn't go to sleep though. I texted Ellie and played my guitar until gone midnight. I'm halfway through composing a song called 'Dad, Dad, You Make Me Mad'.

I click on Dad's text.

I miss you lol x

LOL! Why has he put LOL? Why's he making a joke about leaving me here? Then I remember that Dad thinks that LOL stands for 'lots of love'. I give a massive sigh and press reply.

Miss you too xxx

And I do, even though I'm still mad at him. I miss his stupid jokes and the way the sides of his eyes crinkle when he smiles. I really miss his cooking! But most of all, I miss how he makes me feel safe. My phone bleeps with another message from him.

Don't forget, this isn't forever – just till I've got enough money to get us back on our feet again lol x

I feel a stab of guilt at getting so angry with him.

If he hadn't taken the job in Dubai we would've lost our house.

I know. Don't worry. I'll be fine lol xxx

I can't believe *I'm* using LOL that way now.

My phone instantly chimes with another text – from Ellie this time.

It's probably hunger. I wonder what she'll give you for breakfast!! xxxxx

Somehow I don't think it'll be bacon xoxo

I quickly text back.

I sit up a bit and look around. My bedroom is right at the very top of the building, tucked away in the attic, so the ceiling slopes down on either side. It *looks* really quaint and cosy but it should come with a hazard sign; one with a big red cross and a picture of someone rubbing their head.

Last night, I bumped my head on the ceiling about twenty times just getting ready for bed! The walls are creamy white, and so is the carpet and the duvet cover and the chest of drawers. This room is in serious need of some colour. I'll have to put up some of my photos when I get back from school. *School.* My heart starts pounding again.

It'll be fine, I tell myself. Sometimes, when my inner voice says something wise or comforting like this, I pretend it's Mum speaking to me. I picture her looking down at me, her long blonde hair cascading over her shoulders like Rapunzel's. *It'll be fine.*

I look at the school uniform laid out on the chair by the window. The *tartan* school uniform. How can it be fine when I have to wear tartan?!

'Nessa, are you awake?' Aunt Clara calls up the stairs. 'Breakfast's ready.'

Breakfast is a glass of green paint and a bowl of hamster bedding. Aunt Clara says that it's 'super juice' and 'gluten-free muesli'. I raise the glass to my lips and take the tiniest of sips. The juice tastes like pond water – or how I imagine pond water to taste, anyhow. I force myself to swallow it down. I'm getting really good at that.

'That'll be the spirulina,' Aunt Clara says, looking at me across the table. She's still wearing her dressing gown and her make-up-free face is gleaming with moisturiser. 'It's definitely an acquired taste.'

I thought I'd been able to hide my frown. Obviously not.

'The what?' I ask, not sure if I really want to know.

'It's powdered algae,' Aunt Clara replies with a smile, like drinking powdered algae is something to be happy about. 'It's very good for you, but it does taste a little weird at first.'

'Right.' I want to cry. Why is she making me drink powdered algae? No wonder there was no one in her café yesterday if this is the kind of thing she has on the menu.

Aunt Clara puts down her glass and looks at me, concerned. 'Are you OK? Would you like something else?'

My stomach starts churning with anxiety and fear and for a moment I feel like

I might pass out. I grip on to the table to try and take a deep breath.

'No – I – it's OK. I think I'd better go and get ready for school.'

I'd been hoping that by setting off early for Fairhollow High School I'd avoid seeing any other students but there are already a few tartan-clad clusters of them about. I keep my head down, like I've suddenly become fascinated by the paving slabs. I think of Ellie, all the way down in London, and I feel an aching pain in the pit of my stomach. I fumble in my blazer pocket for Mum's locket and grip it tightly. I'd known that coming here was going to be tough, but I hadn't realised how emotional it was going to make me feel. I take a deep breath of the cold air and slowly exhale. Even though I know Dad is right and supernatural stuff is super-stupid, I secretly hope that Mum *is* somehow with me as I carry on along the road.

When I get to the entrance to Fairhollow High I do a double take in shock. It looks more like a country estate than a school. Set back in beautiful grounds, the winding road up to it is lined by a thick wall of trees. There's even a chapel. I stop for a moment to take it all in before following the signs to reception.

The inside of the school is just as old-fashioned and ornate as the outside, with oak panelling on the walls and dark polished floors as shiny as conkers. I make my way over to the reception desk, my heart pounding.

'Hi, I'm Nessa Reid,' I say to the woman sitting behind the desk. She has pale grey hair pinned up in a bun and she's wearing gold-rimmed, half-moon glasses. She stares at me over the glasses for a second before a flicker of recognition crosses her face.

'Ah, yes! Our new girl. Clara Hamilton's niece.' She looks me up and down as if she's trying to decide what to make of me, then finally she smiles. 'Now, what form did we put you in?' She starts looking through a huge leather-bound book on the desk in front of her. 'Ah, yes. Mr Matthews, Year Eight.'

Just as she says this, two girls and a boy come clattering through the front doors, laughing loudly. I can tell instantly from looking at them that they're popular kids. One of the girls has white-blonde hair falling down to her shoulders in loose curls, the other has poker-straight brown hair fashionably pulled back into a ponytail. They both look as if they've just sashayed off a catwalk. They're even managing to make their kilts look cool. The boy has one of those film-star faces, all chiselled cheekbones and gleaming teeth. I guess he must be the boyfriend of one of the girls — the blonde one's, probably.

The brown-haired girl looks way too haughty to have a boyfriend. She reminds of the Evil Queen in *Snow White*. They all glance over at me curiously and I pretend to look for something in my bag.

'Ah! Izzy, Vivien, Stephen!' the receptionist calls. 'Would you take Nessa here upstairs with you? She's starting in your form today.'

There's a moment's silence. All I can hear is a pounding in my head.

'Sure,' the blonde girl finally replies. Her voice is crisp and polished. I look up from my bag. They're all still staring at me. None of them are smiling.

'Thank you, Izzy,' the receptionist trills before turning back to her work.

I trudge over to them.

'Hi, I'm Nessa,' I mumble.

'Yes, we got that,' the girl with dark hair – she must be Vivien – says curtly. They start walking off down the corridor. I trail after them, feeling red-hot with a mixture of embarrassment and anger.

25

They could at least be trying to make conversation. When we get to a stairwell at the end of the corridor the blonde girl Izzy looks back over her shoulder at me. I smile at her, but she turns away, and I feel a sudden chill run right through me. It's really strange – like I'm shivering on the inside of my body.

I follow them up two flights of stairs and past a row of doors to the end of a corridor. They still don't say anything to me, just open the door and go through. I check the sign on the door just to make sure they haven't brought me to the wrong place for a prank, but the sign says *Mr Matthews, 8MA*.

As it's still so early, there's only a handful of other students in the form room when I go in. Mr Matthews is sat behind his desk marking a pile of books. He's old and stick thin, with crazy wiry white hair springing from his head. I go and stand by his desk, but he's so engrossed in his marking that he doesn't notice me. I cough and he still doesn't look up. My face starts to burn.

'New girl, sir,' Stephen shouts suddenly, causing Mr Matthews to jump. He looks at me at last and frowns.

'New girl?'

I nod. 'Yes, sir. Nessa Reid.'

Mr Matthews's pale blue eyes light up. 'Of course! Clara Hamilton's niece.' He stands up and promptly knocks his pile of books over. 'Welcome, welcome,' he says as he tries to put it back together. 'I used to know your mother, Celeste. I taught her, actually – many moons ago. You look so like her it's uncanny.' His smile fades and he shakes his head. 'I was so sorry when I heard – you know – when she died.'

I nod and look away.

'OK, we need to find someone to take care of you until you've found your feet,' Mr Matthews says. 'We don't want you ending up going for lunch in the gymnasium now, do we?' He laughs heartily at his own joke and scans the classroom. *Please, please, please don't say Izzy, Stephen or Vivien*, I silently beg.

27

'Izzy!' Mr Matthews says. 'Can you take Nessa under your wing for the next few days – show her where everything is? Make her feel welcome.'

I reluctantly turn round to look at her. I'm expecting a glare, but to my surprise, Izzy is smiling.

'Of course, sir.' Izzy beckons to me. 'Come and sit here, Nessa. I'll make sure you're OK.'

I hear someone to the left of me cough. It's the kind of pointed cough that's trying to say something. I turn and see a girl with dark skin and curly dark brown hair hunched over her desk, her face buried behind a book.

I pick up my bag and head over to Izzy. She's still smiling at me. But I'm not sure I like it. For some reason it reminds me of the smile the big bad wolf gave Little Red Riding Hood – right before he tried to gobble her up.

My morning hanging out with Izzy, Vivien and Stephen turns out to be totally weird and really exhausting. Everywhere they go, the other students either stare at them in awe or suck up to them like they're mega-famous celebrities. And because Izzy is still being creepily super-friendly to me, the other students have all been treating me the same way. I feel like a singer who's just found overnight stardom after years of singing songs into her hairbrush in her bedroom. It all feels kind of surreal given how unfriendly they were to me first thing this morning. I'd thought that as soon as registration was over and we were away from Mr Matthews, they'd go straight back to blanking me. But if anything, it's been the opposite. Izzy made

Vivien sit with Stephen in every single lesson this morning so that I could sit next to her. And Vivien didn't even seem to really mind. She hasn't been as super-smiley to me as Izzy has, but scowling just seems to be her default setting.

Izzy told me to meet them in the canteen for lunch, but as soon as the bell goes, I head to the toilets. I need some time on my own to process everything that's happened this morning. I lock the cubicle door, shut the toilet lid and sit down. I've never had loads of friends at school and I've definitely never been part of the 'cool group', so I don't know how to handle this. My friendship with Ellie has always been enough for me. I take my phone out of my blazer pocket I'm glad to see a new text message from her.

How's it going? I MISS YOU!!! ☹ xxxx

As I read it I feel a sharp pain again, as if a giant fist is clenching my stomach. I press reply.

**It's been really weird – I seem to have been
adopted by the populars and I can't work out
why!! I MISS YOU TOO!!! xxxx**

The door to the toilets bangs open and someone
goes into the cubicle next to mine. I take a deep
breath and put my phone back in my pocket.,
Although it's been unnerving hanging out with
Izzy, Vivien and Stephen, I guess it's better than
having to drift around all day on my own. I pick up
my bag and head off for lunch.

Even though the canteen's really crowded,
it's easy to spot Izzy's white-blonde hair. They're
sitting at a table at the back with a girl who's from
our form. She has very short hair and huge glasses.
She looks really sweet and shy and this instantly
makes me feel better. I think I'll feel way more
relaxed if I can chat to her. But as I get closer to the
table I get hit by a sudden and completely random
feeling of fear. Izzy's leaning in close to the girl,
looking like she's whispering a secret in her ear. But

whatever she's saying can't be nice – the girl looks really upset.

'It looks like your mum just put a bowl on your head and started cutting,' I hear Vivien say to her just as I reach the table.

'Couldn't you afford to get a proper haircut?' Izzy says.

'Maybe I should shave it all off with my dad's clippers,' Stephen adds, sneering. 'It couldn't look any worse.'

I'm frozen to the spot. There's no way I want to sit with them now if this is how they treat people, but I don't want to leave the girl on her own with them either. But before I can decide what to do, Izzy spots me.

'Nessa! Come and join us. Eve was just going, weren't you, Eve?' She turns and gives the girl a cold stare.

Eve has a full plate of spaghetti Bolognese in front of her, but she nods and picks up her tray.

'Are you OK?' I ask as Eve shuffles past me.

'Yes, fine,' she mutters without looking at me at all.

'Come on, sit down,' Izzy says, smiling up at me.

Reluctantly, I sit down next to her, still staring at Eve. I think about going after her but I don't know what I'd say. I watch as she scrapes her lunch into a bin before heading out of the canteen. I feel really sick.

'Did you bring lunch, or are you getting something here?' Vivien asks.

My heart sinks as I think of the Tupperware box Aunt Clara gave me this morning. I didn't dare ask her what was in it.

'I brought it,' I mutter, taking the box from my bag. It's full of brown rice and vegetables and weird white cubes. I think they might be cheese, but when I try one it's tasteless and as chewy as rubber. I look up to see Izzy, Stephen and Vivien all staring at me. My face flushes.

'What's that white stuff?' Stephen asks, nodding

at my lunch. I wonder if he's going to start teasing me the way he was teasing Eve and I feel a hot burst of anger. If he does, I decide, I'll shove whatever this stupid lunch is right into his smug face.

'I'm not sure,' I reply, my face burning even hotter.

'You don't know what you've got for lunch?' Vivien asks.

'No.' I stare back at her.

'I think it's tofu,' Izzy says with another smile. 'It looks delicious.'

I look at her, feeling a weird mixture of gratitude and disbelief.

'Thank you,' I mutter. 'My aunt made it. She's vegan.'

Izzy nods. 'Your aunt runs the vegan café in town, doesn't she?'

'Yes. Paper Soul.'

Izzy just keeps on smiling, like she's on some kind of sponsored grinathon. 'I haven't been into Paper Soul for ages. We'll have to have lunch there one weekend, won't we guys?'

Stephen and Vivien nod but they don't seem quite so keen.

I glance at the table in front of ours. The girl from our class with the dark curly hair is staring at me over the book she's reading. When we make eye contact she gives a quick smile before looking back down at her book. I look around and see loads of other students glancing over too. I take a deep breath and force myself to eat another cube of white rubber.

By the time the bell rings for the end of the day my mouth is aching from making myself smile and my entire body is stiff with tension. I have to get out of here. As I shove my books into my bag I look up and see the girl with the dark curly hair staring at me again. It's definitely different to the stares I've been getting from the other students; she's looking at me like she knows me, or knows something about me. I hoist my bag over my shoulder and head over to the door of our form room. Izzy calls out after me but I pretend not to hear her. I need fresh air and I need to be on my own. I'm all new-peopled-out. As I rush along the corridor, I hear the other classroom doors opening behind me and students spilling out. I race down the stairs and through reception. It's only when I get out on to the driveway that I start feeling calmer again.

'Nessa! Wait!'

My throat tightens at the sound of Izzy's voice.

I turn and see all three of them running to catch up with me. What is wrong with them? Why are they so desperate to hang out with me? It's obvious I'm not in their league – this is going against all the natural laws of the school feeding chain.

'Why did you race off like that?' Izzy says, catching me up. Her pale cheeks have flushed pink, making her look even more like a porcelain doll.

'I don't know,' I mutter.

'Do you want to come and hang out at mine?' she asks. 'We were going to go in the pool.'

'The pool?'

Izzy nods. 'Yes. Don't worry. It's indoors and it's heated.'

'Oh, well,' I rack my brains for an excuse. 'I – I don't have a swimming costume.'

Izzy grins. 'That's OK. You can borrow one of mine.'

My insides start crawling with embarrassment. It's been bad enough having to hang out with new people all day without them seeing me semi-naked. And something tells me Izzy's the kind of girl who would own only the skimpiest bikinis.

'Come on, it'll be fun.' Izzy links arms with me.

I automatically pull away. 'I'm really sorry. I can't. I have to – I have to help my aunt, in the café.'

Izzy sighs. For a moment I think I've managed to wriggle out of it, but then she starts smiling again. 'We could come with you – hang out there for a while.'

I look at the others hoping they'll disagree, but

37

even Stephen's nodding.

'You can't!' I say, way too forcefully.

'What do you mean, we can't?' Vivien asks, icily.

'It's not open today,' I stammer. 'I'm helping my aunt do a stock check.'

Izzy stares at me for a moment, like she's not sure whether to believe me. 'Wow, your eyes,' she says at last.

'What about them?'

'I swear they were pale blue this morning. Now they look really dark.'

'It's just the light,' I say. People have said this about my eyes before. I guess they're just a weird shade of blue that looks different in different settings. 'Anyway, I'd better get going.'

Izzy looks at me for a moment, then she nods. 'OK. See you tomorrow.'

'Yes. See you tomorrow.' I pull up the hood on my coat and start walking, my heart pounding in time with my feet.

*

As soon as I've got away from the populars, I start feeling better. The icy air feels lovely and fresh after the stuffy, overheated classrooms. I don't feel ready to go back to Paper Soul just yet and face trying to make conversation with Aunt Clara, so when I get to the crossroads instead of turning left on to the High Street I go straight on. I follow the road round a corner and see a footpath leading up into the woods. It looks so quiet and peaceful that I feel drawn to it like a magnet. As I head in among the trees all I can hear are the chirps of birds as they flying to roost for the night. It's so soothing after the all the yelling and clattering of school. I take a deep breath. The air smells of a beautiful mixture of woodsmoke and damp pine. I follow the footpath up the hill until I come to a huge old oak tree. Its roots are gnarled, pushing up through the icy ground like a pair of giant arms. I nestle down in a nook between them and lean back against the huge trunk. It feels as if the tree is hugging me and slowly I start to relax. I've survived my first day at Fairhollow High. I take Mum's locket from my pocket and trace my fingers over the star.

It's weird to think that I'm now living in the town that Mum grew up in, going to the same school she went to, and with the same teacher. Weird but nice. Imaginary scenes start playing in my head. Mum walking down the High Street. Mum going to school. Mum sitting at a desk listening to Mr Matthews take the register. Mum walking and playing in these woods, maybe even around this tree. My body starts filling with a warm glow. Hopefully, coming to Fairhollow will help me get to know her better. Whenever I asked Dad to tell me about her he'd just close up and mutter, 'I can't', so I gave up trying. But I'm living with Aunt Clara now. Surely she'll be able to tell me loads once she's got used to me being here. Scrambling to my feet, I decide to go back to Paper Soul and give it a try.

4

The next morning, as I make my way to school, I feel way better than I did yesterday. Last night with Aunt Clara was actually quite relaxed. When I asked her if she could tell me more about Mum she went and got an old chocolate box filled with photos of her and Mum as little kids. We spent ages going through the pictures, with Aunt Clara telling me the story behind each one. She's even given me one of the pictures to keep. It's of Mum when she was the same age as me. Looking at it is kind of spooky. We're so similar we could be twins.

As I walk through the school gates I picture

Aunt Clara and Mum when they were my age, walking along the driveway in front of me. I imagine Mum swinging her bag and Aunt Clara nibbling on a carrot or some other root vegetable. Even though it was years ago, re-tracing Mum's footsteps like this gives me a warm glowy feeling that lasts all the way to my form room.

'Hey, Nessa!' Izzy calls to me as soon as I walk through the door.

The girl with the dark curly hair is sat at the front hunched over a book again. She looks up at me and raises her eyebrows. I'm feeling so much more relaxed today that I actually smile at her. She looks surprised then quickly smiles back before returning to her reading.

'Come and sit here,' Izzy calls.

Although I'm not too keen on hanging around with Izzy and the others again, I guess it's less hassle to be in with the popular gang than in their bad books.

The final lesson before lunch is History. We're

learning about Henry VIII. It's a lesson I've already done in my old school so it's pretty boring, until the teacher, Miss Maxwell asks if anyone has any questions. The girl with the dark curly hair, who has so far been silent in all of the lessons I've had with her, puts up her hand.

'Yes, Holly,' Miss Maxwell says.

'Why do we have to spend so much time studying a psycho wife abuser?' Holly asks.

Izzy sighs but I can't help grinning. I've never got why school makes such a huge deal of Henry VIII either.

'I mean, it's not as if there aren't like, a ton of other people – a ton of other way more inspirational women – we could study,' Holly continues.

'Shut up, idiot,' Stephen mutters behind me, making me want to turn round and scowl at him.

'There's Joan of Arc and Boudicca and –'

'OK, thank you, Holly,' Miss Maxwell interrupts. 'Anyone else got any questions related to Henry VIII?'

'My question *was* related to Henry VIII,' Holly says indignantly.

Eve puts her hand up but the bell goes before she can say anything and the room is filled with the clatter of chairs.

As we go to leave, Miss Maxwell calls Izzy back to talk to her about her homework. I seize the opportunity to escape out the door, and Holly is right next to me.

'Hi,' she says.

'Hi,' I say back.

'So, how are you finding it here?'

'OK.' I summon up the courage to give a reply of more than two syllables. 'I liked what you said just then in class. I don't know why we study him either.'

Holly looks at me like she thinks I might be tricking her. 'Really?'

I nod.

She starts to grin and her brown eyes twinkle. 'Do you want to have lunch with me?'

'Yes, please!' I'm so relieved to have someone other than Izzy and her gang to hang out with that I can barely hide my excitement.

When Holly and I get to the canteen we grab a couple of empty seats at the end of a table.

'So, how come you've moved to Fairhollow?' Holly asks, taking a paper bag from her backpack and placing it on the table in front of her. I watch enviously as she takes out two huge sausage rolls.

'I'm staying with my Aunt Clara while my dad's away working in Dubai.'

As Holly takes a bite of one of the sausage rolls, I practically start to drool. I take out my own lunch box. Maybe it'll be something nicer today. But as soon as I open it, my heart sinks. It's full of little round orange things and a ton of chopped vegetables.

'How long's your dad away for?' Holly asks.

'His contract's for a year, but he'll be home for holidays and stuff.' I take a mouthful of the orange things. They taste so weird I can't help grimacing.

'What is that?' Holly asks, but unlike Stephen yesterday, she seems genuinely interested.

'I'm not exactly sure. My aunt's vegan,' I explain. I take another mouthful but it's no good – I can't make myself like it.

'Oh. Well, would you like one of my sausage rolls then?'

Normally, if a virtual stranger offered me some of their lunch, I'd be polite and say no, but I'm way too hungry and the sausage roll looks way too nice.

'Yes, please, if you're sure.'

'Sure I'm sure.' She hands me one of the sausage rolls. I take a huge bite. Holly looks at my lunch. 'Can I try some of yours in exchange?'

'Of course!' I practically shove the box at her.

'Oh, this is really good,' Holly says, as she takes a forkful.

'Really?' I stare at her.

'Mmm. I love the different flavours. Oh, I miss home-cooked food.' She gives a dramatic sigh. 'Shall we just do a total swap?' She pushes the other sausage roll towards me. I nod and grab it eagerly. This lunch break could not be going better.

But then I see Izzy, Stephen and Vivien appear in the doorway. Izzy scans the canteen. As soon as she sees me she smiles, but then she sees Holly and her smile wilts into a frown. She nudges the others and leads them over to me.

'Nessa, what are you doing?' she says.

'Having lunch.'

'With her?' Izzy scowls at Holly.

'Yes.' I glance across the table at Holly. Suddenly I'm hit by a wave of sickness.

'Right.' Izzy smiles at me again, but I can tell from the cold look in her eyes that she doesn't mean it. A shiver runs right the way up my spine. 'Come on,' she says to the others, and they go and sit at the table next to ours.

I look at Holly apologetically, still feeling really queasy. 'I'm sorry. Mr Matthews told Izzy to take care of me and she's taking it very seriously.'

Holly makes a sarcastic noise. 'Yeah, that's Izzy, all heart.' She takes another forkful of Aunt Clara's lunch. 'So, what about your mum? Where's she?'

I look down at the table. 'My mum's – she died.'

Holly instantly puts her fork down. 'Oh no. I'm so sorry, I didn't realise.'

'It's OK, it was a long time ago.'

'But it must be really hard for you, especially now your dad's away.'

The concern in Holly's voice makes me feel really good. The entire time I was with Izzy and the others yesterday they barely asked me a question about myself. It's so nice being with someone who genuinely cares – almost like being with Ellie again.

'Yes, it is a bit, but I've got Aunt Clara.'

Holly glances over at Izzy's table and I get that sick scared feeling again. What's wrong with me? Ever since I've arrived in Fairhollow it's as if I've been on some kind of emotional roller coaster. I can't wait till things settle down and I can start feeling normal again.

'Can I ask you something?' Holly looks all serious.

I nod. 'Of course.'

'How do you feel about Izzy and the others?' Holly asks. 'Do you like them? Do you want to hang out with them?' She studies my face like she's searching for some kind of clue.

'Not really. I mean, I'm grateful that they looked after me yesterday, but I don't think they're the kind of people I'd choose as friends.'

Holly grins so hard a pair of dimples appear either side of her mouth. 'Well, you know, if you want someone else to hang out with there's always me.' She looks down at the lunch box shyly. 'I mean, I don't really care if you do or you don't, but if you do . . .'

'I do. Thank you.' The warm glow inside of me is suddenly replaced by a cold chill of dread. I look up to see Izzy, Stephen and Vivien standing by our table again.

'Come on, Nessa, let's go back to our form room,' Izzy says.

I look at Holly and my stomach lurches. She's gazing down into her lap.

'It's OK, you guys go ahead. I'll come up with Holly,' I say.

Izzy leans down closer to me, so close I can smell her perfume. It's really unusual, spicy and strong. 'We need to go now,' she says in a loud firm voice. 'I don't know why you're hanging out with a freak like her anyway. You could have had lunch with us.'

I stare up at her, my heart pounding. Who does she think she is, telling me what to do? There's a definite hush from the tables closest to us as everyone waits to see how I'm going to respond.

'I said no,' I say in an equally loud, firm voice. 'I'll come up when I've finished my lunch – with Holly.'

Izzy stares at me.

I stare back. I don't need her friendship. Who wants to hang out with a control freak like that?

Izzy takes a sharp breath in and her cheeks flush bright pink. Silence spreads across the canteen as we continue to stare at each other. Finally, she tosses her hair over her shoulder, turns and marches away.

Stephen and Vivien go scuttling after her.

Reasons why sitting next to Holly in class is way better than sitting with Izzy:

She is really interesting,

She seems genuinely interested in me,

She is *so* much more fun.

Here's an example of how much fun. When we were the first ones to get to our Geography lesson, Holly slipped up to the teacher's desk and covered the end of his whiteboard pen with red ink. 'I'm not mean to all teachers,' she whispered to me as she sat back down, 'just the fascist dictators. And Mr Groddle is a definite fascist dictator.'

Mr Groddle, it turns out, is one of those

teachers who likes being mean to kids at every opportunity. He also likes tapping his face with the end of his whiteboard pen while he waits for the answer to one of his questions. So, by the end of the lesson, his face is covered in red marks, and I can barely breathe from holding my laughter in.

At the end of the day, Mr Matthews asks me to stay behind to ask me how I'm getting on. Holly waits for me like it's the natural thing to do and this makes me so happy and grateful I want to dance. Somehow, I manage to hold my happiness in as we stroll out of school together. As we walk down the driveway, feathery snowflakes start drifting down from the sky.

'I love winter,' Holly says, tipping her head back and sticking out her tongue to catch a snowflake. 'It's so pretty *and* it's hot chocolate season.' She looks at me hopefully. 'Do you want to go and get a hot chocolate at The Cup and Saucer? Or we could go to your aunt's café?'

I frown. 'I don't think she does hot chocolate.'

Holly looks at me, horrified.

'It's a vegan café. Vegans don't drink milk.'

'Oh right! The Cup and Saucer it is, then.' She rummages in her book-filled backpack for her phone. 'I've just got to text Svetlana to let her know I'll be a bit late home.'

'Who's Svetlana?'

Holly's face crinkles into a frown. 'She's my au pair.'

I look at her, puzzled. Surely Holly's a little old to have an au pair.

'My parents work away a lot,' Holly says as she texts. 'They're lawyers – for an international law firm – so they get to fly around the world working on swanky cases together. Svetlana lives in our house and looks after me while they're away – when she's not on Skype to her family back in Russia, or having crazy arguments with her boyfriend, or out at her amateur dramatics society.' Holly finishes texting and puts her phone back in her bag. 'Basically, I barely see her and that suits me just fine.'

I feel a tug of sadness as I think of Holly

being left with an au pair. No wonder she was so understanding when I told her about my parents.

'Do you miss your parents when they're away?'

Holly shrugs her thin shoulders. 'Not really. I'm used to it. And I'll see them for the whole of Christmas when we go on holiday, the three of us.'

We reach the end of the driveway and turn on to the road.

'But don't you get lonely?'

'No!' Holly stares at me like I'm crazy. 'Why would I get lonely when I've got books? They're always there, and they never tell me to tidy my room or go to bed.'

I start laughing. 'Good point.'

I hear the sound of voices coming from the other side of the road. I look across and see the entrance to a park. A group of Fairhollow High students are gathered in a copse of trees, sheltering from the snow. In the fading light I can't make out who they are but I see one of them get to her feet and start running over.

'Nessa!'

My heart sinks at the sound of Izzy's voice. The others drift over behind her.

'Nessa, what are you doing?' Izzy stares pointedly at Holly.

I frown at her. 'Going home?'

'But why are you walking with *Holly*?' Izzy spits out Holly's name like it's poisonous.

'Because I want to.' The others have reached us now and they all gather around. There's Vivien and Stephen of course, and a group of other hangers-on, all gazing at Izzy to see what she'll say next.

But it's Vivien who steps forward. 'Holly's a freak,' she says loudly, causing a couple of the hangers-on to start giggling. Izzy watches icily. 'Why would you want to hang out with her?'

'Who are you calling a freak?' Holly says, taking a step towards Vivien.

'You, you little saddo,' Vivien smirks, shoving Holly's shoulder. Holly stumbles backwards.

Now I'm mad. So mad I find myself squaring

up to Vivien. 'Don't you dare! You're pathetic – all of you.' I look around at the others and then back at Vivien and Izzy. 'Leave us alone.' For some strange reason I don't feel at all scared. It's like my anger has formed a force field around me.

Izzy's green eyes go cold. 'So you've made your choice?' she says quietly.

I stare at her. Why's she being so melodramatic? 'Yes, I've made my choice.'

'You're really going to regret this,' Izzy hisses.

'I don't think so.'

Izzy's eyes narrow. 'Oh, you will.'

Stephen leans in close to Izzy. 'What are you doing?' I hear him whisper to her.

Izzy turns back towards the park. 'Come on, we're going.'

Stephen looks at me, then at Izzy again. 'But . . .'

'But nothing!' Izzy hisses, walking away.

Vivien automatically follows her. Stephen watches me carefully for a minute and then goes after her too.

The hangers-on all look really confused. I guess they're not used to seeing their leader so ruffled. One by one they follow her back into the park, disappearing into the growing darkness.

I turn back to Holly.

'Are you OK?'

She nods, but she looks really upset. She leans against a lamppost. Then there's a massive bang, like a crack of thunder, and the bulb blows.

I look up at the lamppost in shock. 'Wow! What made it do that?'

Holly looks shaken. 'Er – it's probably an old bulb. Let's get out of here.' She picks up her bag and starts heading off towards the High Street.

'What's Izzy's problem?' I ask, running to keep up with her. 'Why's she so controlling?'

Holly shrugs and keeps walking. 'I don't know.'

'I just don't get why she's so keen for me to hang out with them. Hasn't she got enough fans? I mean, seriously.'

But Holly doesn't say a word. I guess she's still

shaken up by what happened.

Anxiety starts bubbling up in the back of my throat. I swallow it down. 'I'm sorry. I feel like I've caused a load of trouble for you.'

Holly stops dead and shakes her head. 'Don't be stupid. It's not your fault. It's them. I really like you.'

'Really?'

She looks at me, her dark brown eyes deadly serious. 'Yes. You called Izzy pathetic. It was just like when Aslan stands up to the White Witch in *The Lion, the Witch and the Wardrobe*. It was epic!' She starts to smile and I feel a surge of relief. Even though what just happened with Izzy has really upset me, I feel happier than I have since getting to Fairhollow. Holly likes me. I've made a real friend at last.

'Vanessa, my darling, how are you?!' Ellie cries from my laptop screen in her best posh actress voice.

'Wonderful, Eleanor, darling,' I cry back. 'Fabulous, in fact.'

It's Saturday morning and we're Skyping. We like to begin our Skype calls talking like posh actresses. It makes us laugh. I'm trying to pretend that it's just the same as Ellie being in the room, but it's not. Seeing her face on my computer makes it feel as if she's being beamed in from another planet. She's so far away, she might as well be.

'Well, I'm OK . . .' I say in my normal voice. 'It's

definitely getting better.' And it is, apart from Izzy and her minions looking at me like I'm carrying some kind of deadly disease all the time. I've settled into my classes and Holly and I have been getting on really well. I'm not sure how to tell Ellie about Holly, though. It feels a bit weird, like I've been cheating on our friendship.

'That's great,' Ellie leans back in her desk chair and smiles.

I catch glimpses of her room behind her – the fairy lights strung across the headboard on her bed, the white shelves lining the wall, crammed full of trinkets and DVDs, the clothes spilling from her chest of drawers. I glance around at my room. It's still a bland sea of cream. I can't wait to get some bits and pieces to brighten it up.

'You'll never guess what happened in Gym yesterday,' Ellie says, and as she fills me in on all the latest news from London, I feel really sad. It's like I'm looking in on my old life, no longer able to be a part of it. 'So, what are you doing this weekend?'

'Nothing much. I'm going shopping in a bit.'

'With your aunt?'

'No.' I pause. 'With a girl from school. Holly.'

'Oh. That's nice.' Ellie's smile falters.

'I wish I was going shopping with you,' I say quietly.

'Me too.'

We both look at each other and for a moment it doesn't feel as if we're Skyping, it feels as if we're face to face.

'You'll always be my best friend,' I say.

'Yes,' Ellie says firmly. 'Always.'

I feel a wave of relief.

'Just think how cool it will be when we do get to see each other again,' Ellie says with a grin.

'It'll be awesome. We'll need an entire week to catch up on everything.'

'Shall we Skype again tomorrow?' Ellie says.

'Yes. Definitely.'

We say goodbye and I start getting ready to go into town. I can't decide what to wear so I look out of the window for inspiration. The sky is chalk white again but it feels a bit warmer than it has been and there's only a thin dusting of snow on the rooftops opposite. I pull on a pair of black jeans and a dark grey hoodie. Holly and I have arranged to meet outside The Cup and Saucer. The thought of it makes me suddenly feel squirmy with shyness. I've got used to hanging out with Holly in school but this will be the first time we've gone shopping together. I sit down on my bed and sigh. I can't wait until we're past all of these firsts and I don't have to stress any more.

Downstairs in the café, Aunt Clara is sat at one of the tables talking to Dawn, a woman with bright pink hair and a unicorn tattoo who works in the café on Saturdays.

'Ah, Nessa, we were just talking about you,' Aunt Clara says.

'Oh?'

'Yes, we were wondering if maybe you'd like some work in the run-up to Christmas, to earn a few extra pounds. We could do with a hand, with the Christmas rush.'

I look around the deserted shop and try not to raise my eyebrows. 'That would be great. Thank you.' I walk round to the front of the counter.

'Where are you off to today?' asks Aunt Clara.

'Shopping with my friend from school. I want to get some things for my bedroom, to make it look a bit more – homely.'

As soon as I say it I feel a pang of regret. I hope Aunt Clara doesn't think I'm being rude. But she smiles at me and gets up and comes over to the counter. 'Lovely.' She takes some money from her purse and hands it to me. 'Here, for your bedroom things.'

'Oh, no – I have some money Dad gave me.'

Aunt Clara shakes her head and places the money in my hand. 'I want you to have it. I want you to feel at home. I'm really pleased you've made a new friend too.' She keeps hold of my hand for a second and looks me straight in the eyes. A sensation of warmth rushes through my body, right down to the tips of my toes.

'Thank you.'

I put the money into my pocket and make my way over to the door.

'See you later,' I call over my shoulder as I go.

As I get close to The Cup and Saucer, I see Holly at one of the tables outside, her coat collar pulled up against the cold. She's engrossed in a book. As soon as she glances up and sees me she starts to smile, and I get that same warm feeling I got when Aunt Clara gave me the money. There's no doubt about it, moving to Fairhollow has made me super-emotional.

'Ness!' Holly cries as she gets to her feet. 'It's so good to see you.' She gestures at the High Street. 'Though we're not exactly on Oxford Street, I'm afraid.'

I shrug. 'That's fine. I hate Oxford Street. It's way too crowded.'

'Ha, well you definitely won't get that problem here.'

I follow Holly's gaze up the High Street. The only people in sight are an elderly couple coming out of the butcher's and a mum pushing a pram.

'I need to get some things for my bedroom,' I say to Holly. 'Some things to brighten it up a bit; make it more homely. Some cushions maybe?'

Holly furrows her brow in thought, then her eyes light up. 'We need to go to Home & Glory,' she says, swinging her backpack over her shoulder. 'Come on, you'll love it.'

Home & Glory is tucked away down a side street between a florist's and an undertaker's. It's three storeys high just like Paper Soul, but the shop is spread across all three floors, with little nooks and crannies stuffed full of quirky home stuff. I end up buying a dark plum-coloured throw, some silvery satin cushions and a string of half-moon-shaped fairy lights. I also secretly buy Holly a pair of bookends shaped like elephants after I get the strongest feeling she would like them.

When we get back outside, I give them to her.

'To say thank you,' I say, feeling suddenly embarrassed.

'What for?' Holly asks, her brown eyes wide with surprise.

'For being my friend.'

Holly tears off the tissue paper like a little kid unwrapping a Christmas present. 'Oh my God! I love these. I wanted to get them myself but I've spent the last of my pocket money. Thank you!' Her eyes look like they've filled with tears. 'You don't have to thank me at all,' she says quietly. Then she grins. 'I mean, who wouldn't want to be friends with someone who lives in a bookshop? Please, please, please, can we go there next?'

I laugh. 'Of course. Although I have to warn you, you might not like it – it's not exactly like other bookshops.'

Holly frowns. 'I've peeped in before. It's got books in it, right?'

'Yes.'

'Then I like it.'

We make our way back down the High Street, laughing and joking, I feel so thankful to be doing something like this, something as normal as going Saturday morning shopping with a friend. When we get to Paper Soul I even feel a pang of affection for it. To my surprise there are quite a few people in the shop now, browsing through the books.

'Oh, this is so cool,' Holly sighs as she looks around. 'It's exactly how a bookshop should be.'

I stare at her in surprise. 'Really?'

Holly nods. 'Yes. I love the way it's set out, with the reading chairs in the corners. You can tell it's owned by a true book lover.'

Aunt Clara emerges from one of the alcoves, holding a stack of books.

'Nessa,' she cries when she see me, smiling widely. 'How did you get on? Oh!' As soon as she sees Holly her smile fades.

'This is my new friend from school – Holly,' I say.

Holly grins at Aunt Clara. 'Hi. I love your shop.'

'Yes. Well . . .' Aunt Clara stands motionless, staring from me to Holly and back again.

'Would it be OK if Holly comes up to my room for a bit?' I ask.

Aunt Clara frowns. 'I'm afraid not. I – er – I need your help with something.'

'What?' Why's she acting so weird?

Aunt Clara looks down at the floor. 'Do you remember me saying this morning about you helping out in the shop?'

'Yes, but I thought you said I didn't need to start till next week.' I stare at her.

'I could help too,' Holly says eagerly. 'Especially if it's anything to do with books. Books are my speciality,' she adds with a grin.

'Thank you, but I'm afraid I just need Nessa.' Aunt Clara's reply is so blunt I stare at her in shock.

I don't understand what's going on here. The anxious feelings I'd been getting earlier in the week make an unwelcome return to the pit of my stomach.

'Maybe you could come over to mine later?' Holly says to me.

'That won't be possible,' Aunt Clara says before I can get a word in. 'We really do have a lot to get done.' Then she turns and heads towards the café.

'I'm so sorry,' I say to Holly, feeling really anxious now. Why is Aunt Clara being so rude? This is so embarrassing.

Holly sighs. 'That's OK. I guess we'll see each other on Monday then, in school.'

I nod, feeling close to tears.

As soon as Holly's gone my sadness turns to anger. Why's Aunt Clara trying to ruin the one friendship I've got? Doesn't she know how hard it is to make new friends? I storm into the café. Dawn is busy at the counter with a customer. I walk past and into the kitchen at the back. Aunt Clara is leaning against a work unit with her head in her hands.

'Why were you so rude to Holly?' I say. But as soon as the words leave my mouth my anger's replaced by a wave of anxiety so strong it makes my head spin. What is wrong with me? I grip on to the table and take a deep breath. 'She's really nice and she's made me feel really welcome.'

Aunt Clara mutters something.

'What?'

'It's not Holly, it's just that we've got such a lot on here.' She looks around the kitchen as if she's searching for an excuse. 'I've decided to open on Sunday this weekend . . . for the Christmas shoppers . . . I need you to help me bake some extra cakes.' But there's something about the way she keeps pausing that leaves me sure that she's making it up as she goes along. What's going on?

In the end, it only takes us two hours to make the extra cakes. Two hours of grating beetroot, sifting flour and awkward silence. By the time we've finished there's definitely still enough time for me to go round to Holly's, but I'm too embarrassed and I now have a pounding headache anyway. So I go up to my room and arrange my new things from Home & Glory instead. Usually, I like doing stuff like this. Dad calls me a room fairy because wherever I go in our house I'm lighting candles or fluffing up cushions, trying to make everything look nicer, but today everything I do feels wrong. I can't decide how to arrange the cushions and I don't know where to string the fairy lights. In the end I give up and lie down, staring at the window until the room grows dark and Aunt Clara calls me for dinner.

When I get downstairs she's sitting at the dining room table waiting for me. She's changed into a long burgundy sweater dress and taken off her make-up. Without all of the black eyeliner she looks a lot softer.

As I sit down opposite her I feel a prickle of hope. Maybe she was just stressed out earlier. Maybe now she'll be more understanding.

'Would it be OK if I invite Holly over here tomorrow to hang out for a bit?' I say, unfolding my paper napkin and placing it on my lap.

Aunt Clara's face instantly clouds over. 'Oh no, I don't think so.' She takes the lid off a large dish in the middle of the table. Spirals of steam coil up towards the ceiling.

'Why not?'

Aunt Clara spoons some pasta and vegetables on to my plate. 'I told you – I'm going to be really busy in the shop.'

'But we won't be any trouble. We'll stay in my room.'

Aunt Clara shakes her head.

'Or I could meet her in town again if you don't want us here.'

'It's not that I don't want you here,' Aunt Clara says quickly. 'It's her – she . . .'

'She what?'

'She's trouble,' Aunt Clara says quietly, refusing to make eye contact with me.

73

I stare at her as she starts to eat. 'What do you mean, she's trouble?'

'She's Holly Thornton, right?'

'Yes.'

'I've heard some bad things about her. She's always getting into trouble at school.'

'No she's not! And anyway, I like her!'

Aunt Clara puts her fork down and gives me a tight smile. 'You'll find other people you like. You've only been here a week.'

'Don't remind me.' Sorrow floods my body like a dam bursting. I stumble to my feet before I start to cry. 'I'm going to bed.'

'I'm sorry, Nessa, but I know what's best for you, and I don't want you spending time with that girl.'

I race upstairs, tears burning at my eyes. When I got to my room I throw myself on my bed and hug one of my new cushions tightly. I listen out for Aunt Clara's footsteps following me upstairs. I want her to come rushing in and apologise for being stupid and tell me that of course I can be friends with Holly. But all I hear is scraping from downstairs as she clears away the dishes.

And then I have a truly sickening thought. Maybe Aunt Clara doesn't want me here at all. Maybe that's why she's being so mean. I sit bolt upright. Now I'm not sad any more, I'm really angry. Angry with Aunt Clara for being so horrible about Holly. Angry at Izzy and her stupid friends, and angry at Dad for leaving me here in the first place. Even if we lost our home, at least I'd still be with him and I'd still be in London and with Ellie. I take my phone out and send her a quick text.

Are you free to chat? Xoxo

She texts straight back:

Sorry, just got to the cinema with Helen.
Can I call you tomorrow? Hope you're ok?
Xxxxx

I think of Ellie's new friend Helen slipping into my old life like a thief. It feels as if someone is trying to tear my heart out.

I'm fine, don't worry. Enjoy the film xoxo

I look around the room. And the fact that it's *the* room, not *my* room, makes my eyes fill with tears all over again. I look at the bare walls and the plain chest of drawers and the stupid cream carpet and the tears spill down my cheeks. Then I see my guitar propped against the bed. I pick it up and start strumming a few angry chords. As always, it isn't long before I'm sucked into playing a tune. There's been the start of one lurking in my head all week. Now, finally, the missing notes fall into place and it all comes together. As I hum along I start feeling more in control, and with every chord I play, I feel more and more determined. I don't care what Aunt Clara says. I really like Holly, and Aunt Clara is not going to stop me being friends with her.

7

The weekend was so rubbish that for the first time in my life ever I'm actually relieved when my alarm clock goes off on Monday morning. I rub the sleep from my eyes and fumble around for my guitar. One bonus about being sent to live in a crappy town in the middle of nowhere with an aunt who wants to wreck your friendships and make you eat nothing but vegetables and drink pond water is that it's great inspiration for writing songs. At this rate I'm going to have about ten albums' worth by the end of the year. I switch on my fairy lights and tune my guitar. It's still dark outside and the moon is shining like a silver bauble in the corner of the window. I start gently strumming the guitar and humming the harmony.

My dad thinks I'm some kind of musical genius. Apparently, when I was little and I heard a tune on the TV or radio I'd be able to play it by ear on my recorder. He reckons this puts me in the same league as Mozart and Beethoven. All I know is that when I'm working on a song everything else fades away and time seems to disappear. Even though my alarm clock says half an hour's gone by, it feels like I've only been playing for a couple of seconds when Aunt Clara calls me for breakfast.

Aunt Clara and I are awkwardly friendly throughout breakfast. It definitely helps that breakfast today is porridge with honey, not a trace of pond water in sight. For the first time since I got here, I eat every single bit of my meal.

Aunt Clara glances at my empty bowl and smiles. 'You liked it?' She looks at me hopefully.

I nod. 'Yes, it was lovely. Thank you.' For some

weird reason, I'm filled with a sudden flush of happiness. I don't know why, because now all I can think is, *I have to go to school, and when I get to school I'll see Holly for the first time since Aunt Clara was so rude to her. Can I hang out with her without Aunt Clara knowing? And, worse, what if Holly doesn't want to hang out with me anyway?*

But it turns out that Holly is the least of my worries. As soon as I get into school I feel everyone's eyes on me. But not the curious, star-struck gazes I got when I was hanging out with Izzy, Vivien and Stephen last week. These stares are way colder. I grip Mum's locket and make my way to my form room.

Even though it's not quite time for registration, because it's so freezing outside the room is pretty much full when I get there. Mr Matthews is busy marking books with a pen in each hand and behind each ear. Most people are clustered around tables in groups, chattering and laughing. Holly's the only person sitting on her own. As usual, she's reading a book, her brow furrowed in concentration. I hear a cold laugh from the back of the room and the chattering fades. I don't need to look to know that Izzy, Vivien and Stephen must have noticed me. I take a deep breath and pull out the chair next to Holly's.

'Is it OK if I . . . ?'

Holly looks up and instantly a smile spreads across her face. 'Nessa!' she says, sounding genuinely happy.

I'm so relieved I almost want to cry.

'How was the rest of your weekend?' she asks. 'I hope it wasn't too busy in the shop?'

As I sit down, my relief grows and grows. She doesn't seem bothered at all by the way Aunt Clara spoke to her.

'It was pretty busy.' I look down at my lap. 'I – I'm sorry my aunt was so stressed.'

Holly looks at me blankly. 'Was she? I didn't notice. I'm so glad you're here. I need you to distract me.'

I hear Izzy's laugh again, cutting through the murmur of the form room. I block it out. 'Why? What's wrong?'

Holly sighs. 'I've got the dentist this afternoon. Apparently, I need to have two fillings, although my teeth feel fine to me.' She leans in closer to me. 'Sometimes I think dentists are part of an evil conspiracy. They're like the opposite of the Tooth Fairy. They just want to make money from our teeth.'

I laugh and nod.

The bell for registration rings. Mr Matthews looks up from his marking, all surprised, like he hadn't even realised we were here. 'Oh – good morning!' he says cheerily. 'Let the final week of term commence.'

And even though Vivien mutters something after he calls my name on the register, and even though whatever she mutters makes everyone around her snigger, I don't care. All that matters is that Holly still wants to be my friend.

*

81

At first break, I go to my locker to get my huge Science textbook. As I get there, I see a note pinned to the door. I unfold it and read.

We know your dad isn't really away working. You're just too embarrassed to admit he's in prison.

Although the note is typed, I don't need to scan it for fingerprints to know who's behind it – Izzy. What is her problem? Why can't she just leave me alone? And why has she brought my dad into it? My heart starts to pound and my eyes fill with tears. I try to blink them away but it's no good.

'Nessa, are you OK?'

I look up and see Holly heading down the corridor towards me. I stuff the note into my pocket.

'What is it? What's happened?' she says. She looks so concerned it only makes me want to cry even more. I stumble along the corridor to the toilets and only just make it into a cubicle in time before I burst into tears.

I sit on the floor and press my flushed face

against the cool cubicle wall. What is the matter with me? Why do I keep feeling so weird all the time? This is crazy.

There's a gentle tapping on the cubicle door.

'Nessa, are you OK?'

I haul myself to my feet and unlock the door. Holly looks in cautiously. She's holding out a bunch of paper towels.

I take one wipe away the tears. Then I go over to the sink and splash my face with cold water.

Holly looks at my reflection in the mirror. 'Do you want me to take you to the medical room.'

I shake my head. 'No, I'm not ill. It's – it's this.' I reach into my pocket for the scrunched up note and hand it to her.

As Holly reads it, I'm overcome with anger. How dare Izzy do something like this? How dare she say that about my dad? I grip on to the edge of the sink, my whole body burning up with rage.

What is wrong with me? Why do I keep having such intense mood swings?

'I don't know why she's being such a cow to me,' I say, looking at Holly. 'But the weirdest thing is how stressed it's making me. I'm usually good at shaking things off, but ever since I've got here, I feel so – so intense all the time. Like one minute I'll be so happy I want to sing, the next minute I'm throwing up.'

Holly hands the note back to me. She looks at me for a moment, like she wants to tell me something. Then the bell rings for the end of break. 'Come on,' she says. 'We'd better get to Science.'

I watch as Holly turns and heads to the door. What was I thinking? I should never have told her about my mood swings. My stomach starts churning with despair. What if I lose Holly too?

In Science I have to sit on a different table to Holly, so it's impossible to tell if she's still OK with me or not, and when the bell goes for lunch she has to rush off for her dental appointment. But she does say goodbye to me and she does smile – sort of. So I think things are OK. To stop myself obsessing over exactly *how* Holly smiled – and to avoid Izzy and her minions – I decide to steer clear of the canteen and explore the school grounds instead.

I head off behind the chapel, taking a winding path through the deserted playing fields. I follow the path to a cluster of trees. None of them are as big or as comforting as the old oak tree in the woods, but at least they won't stare at me or say rude things about me. I sit down on the cold grass and take my lunch box from my bag. My stomach feels hollow with hunger. When I find a sandwich inside it makes me stupidly excited. The bread is really dark brown, like, so dark brown it's almost black, but it's a sandwich and the lemony hummus actually tastes quite nice. I lean back against the tree and gaze up at the sky. It's filled with huge clouds, the kind that look like mountain ranges, their tips bruised purple and grey by the wintery sunlight. My phone vibrates in my blazer pocket. I take it out and see a text from Dad.

Just having my dinner and thinking of you.
Love you. Miss you. Lol xxx

Tears fill my eyes but this time they're happy ones. I quickly text him back:

Just having my lunch and thinking of you too! Love you miss you too lol xoxo

I stuff my phone back in my pocket. It doesn't matter what Izzy and the others say about Dad. I know he loves me.

I get back to school feeling determined. If I want Izzy to stop her stupid games, I'm going to have to make her. The first lesson after lunch is Gym. I'm the last one out of the changing room because it takes me ages to unknot the lace on one of my trainers. I race out into the corridor and find Izzy, Vivien and Stephen waiting for me.

'All right, freak?' Izzy says, her eyes narrowing. 'Is it true that your dad's in prison for killing someone?'

My heart starts pounding like someone's hitting the inside of my rib cage with a hammer. 'My dad isn't in prison at all.'

'Yeah, right,' Stephen sneers, his eyes going all

small and piggy. 'That's not what we've heard.'

'You're pathetic,' I snap at them. 'What's wrong? Are your lives so boring you have to invent stories about other people just to have something to do?'

Vivien takes a step towards me. 'We have plenty to do.'

I take a step towards her. 'Oh really? Well, why don't you go and do it then, and leave other people alone?'

'Urgh, look at her freaky eyes, they've changed colour again,' Izzy says, staring at me.

The pounding in my chest is so strong now it's reverberating through my entire body. But I don't feel scared. I feel strong. Really, really strong.

'You are so stupid,' I say, staring right back at her.

For a split second, I'm sure I see a flicker of fear in her eyes.

'Come on, let's go,' she mutters to the others.

'What's wrong? Are you scared?' I can't quite believe these words are actually coming out of my mouth. It's like I've been taken over by some kind of butt-kicking superhero.

Izzy strides off down the corridor, with Stephen running after her like a floppy-haired lapdog. Vivien turns to follow them but I grab hold of her arm. I don't feel angry any more, or upset, I feel almost invincible.

'Let go of me,' she yells.

But before I can say anything, a scene flashes into my head like something from a movie; a grim-faced man, slamming a car door and driving off, and the sound of someone crying. A girl crying. I look at Vivien. *She* isn't crying, she's staring at me and, like Izzy, I'm sure I see a flicker of fear in her eyes. My newfound strength rushes out of me like a turning tide and I let go of her arm.

'Freak!' Vivien spits at me, before running off after the others.

I stand in the corridor, dazed and rubbing my eyes. What just happened?

*

I'm still feeling confused as I trudge out of school later. The sun has already set and the sky is charcoal grey. I can't stop thinking about what happened when I was holding Vivien's arm. Why would I get a picture of a random man flashing into my head? And why did I hear a girl crying? A terrible thought occurs to me. What if the stress of moving here is making me go mad?

'Hey, Nesha.'

I've been so preoccupied I didn't even notice Holly standing by the roadside in the shadow of a tree.

'I can't shpeak properly,' she says, holding the side of her mouth. 'The evil dentisht hash maimed me for life.'

'Oh no, did you have to have an injection?'

Holly nods, glumly.

'What are you doing here?'

'I wanted to shee if you were OK.'

'Really?'

Holly nods again.

The knots of tension in my shoulders loosen.

Holly does still want to be my friend, in spite of what happened this morning. I smile at her gratefully. 'I'm really sorry about earlier. I don't know why I got so sick. So much weird stuff keeps happening . . .' I break off, not sure I should say any more.

Holly looks at me. 'What kind of stuff?'

We start walking off along the road together. I feel a bit more confident now we're not facing each other; a bit more able to say things.

'Since I got here everything seems to affect me more than usual,' I begin. 'I keep getting all of these really strong emotions.' I glance at Holly. She's staring at me intently. 'And then today in Gym I decided to confront Izzy and the others about the note, and something really weird happened.'

'What?' Holly stops walking.

'Well, I went to grab hold of Vivien and I had a kind of a flashback. Only it couldn't have been a flashback because I didn't know the people in it. There was this man slamming a car door, and I could hear a girl crying. It was like – it was like I was having a dream, but I was wide awake.' I take a deep breath. Now Holly's bound to think I'm crazy. I sneak a glance at her. She's looking down, scuffing her foot on the icy pavement. 'It must just be the stress of moving, I guess,' I say, trying to lighten things a bit.

Holly nods. She opens her mouth like she's going to say something. Then she closes it again and looks away. 'Oh well, don't worry about it. There's only four more days left before the holidays,' she says brightly. Her voice sounds a bit too high-pitched. 'Five days till the school dance on Saturday.' Her eyes start flitting around, looking everywhere apart from at me. She seems really nervous, and I feel like kicking myself. It's bad enough that I've been sick in front of her today but now I've told her I've been hallucinating too. No wonder she's freaked out. I feel exhausted from trying to figure so much out so I decide to stop trying and focus really hard on just being normal. I look at her and force myself to smile. 'Yes, five days till the dance.'

Somehow I make it through the week without any more craziness happening. Ever since our run-in before Gym, Izzy and the others seem to have been avoiding me. The worst I've got has been the odd icy stare. So, when Saturday comes, I'm actually looking forward to the school dance. And not just because the others have laid off me. Holly is so hyped that her enthusiasm is infectious. And my Music teacher, Mr Graham, has asked me to compose the playlist for the first hour. Apart from meeting Holly, this has been the best thing that's happened to me since I got to Fairhollow. Making playlists is one of my favourite things of all time. As I pack my bag ready to go over to Holly's on Saturday afternoon I check for about the tenth time that I've got my iPod.

Once I'm ready, I go down into the shop. I wouldn't say that it's packed, but it's way busier than I've ever seen it. All of the tables in the café are taken. Dawn is by one of them, serving bowls of soup, and Aunt Clara is busy slicing bread behind the counter.

'I'm off to go and get ready for the dance at Eve's,' I call over to her, feeling an instant pang of guilt for lying. But what am I supposed to do when she's so dead set against Holly? All week I've been creating a fictional friendship with Eve over breakfast and dinner so I'd have a cover story for going to Holly's today.

Aunt Clara looks up from the bread. Her face is flushed and her eyeliner slightly smudged. 'OK, Nessa, have a lovely time. Don't be back too late.'

'I won't.' I feel a pang of sorrow as I wonder if I will ever be able to be completely relaxed and open with Aunt Clara.

I make my way through the shop and out on to the High Street. It's bustling with Christmas shoppers laden down with bags. Although it's only four o'clock, the sky's already a dark inky blue and the wind is icy cold, like it might snow at any minute. I pull down my hat and hurry on. Holly lives right at the other end of the High Street, in one of the grand old houses I saw when I first arrived in Fairhollow. As I walk up the steps to the front door it seems even huger than it did from the taxi. Down below me, to my right, I can see an orange glow coming from a basement window. Other than that, the house is totally dark. I knock on the door, on a huge brass door knocker shaped like a fox's head. From inside the house I hear the clattering of footsteps. Then the door bursts open and Holly is standing there grinning at me, panting like she's just run a race. Only she can't have just run a race, because she's wearing a scarlet 1920s-style dress with a fringe of beads around the bottom. Her curly hair pinned up into a faux bob.

'I've been teaching myself how to do this really cool dance from the 1920s called the Charleston,' she says, breathlessly. 'Well, *YouTube* has been teaching me how to,' she grins at me.

I laugh and look past her into the hall. 'Wow!' The hallway is bigger than the entire ground floor of Dad's and my house in London. A huge staircase with wrought-iron banisters sweeps up behind Holly.

'Sorry! Come in!' she says, flinging the door wider open and pulling me inside. 'It's freezing out there.'

I step on to the black-and-white chequered floor. Holly flicks a light switch and a huge chandelier above us sparkles into life. I'm aware that my mouth is probably gaping open in awe but I can't help it. 'Wow, Holly, this place is amazing!'

Holly looks around nonchalantly. 'Yeah, it's OK, I suppose. I've lived here all my life so I guess I'm just used to it.' She grabs hold of my hand. 'Come with me, I need to show you something.'

96

She leads me up the huge staircase. Up past the first floor and the second, until we reach the top of the house and into a room at the end of the landing.

The room is huge and filled with antique furniture in dark wood. There are two chests of drawers, a wardrobe and a huge four-poster bed. 'Is this Svetlana's room?' I ask. Holly shakes her head.

'No, it was my grandma's. This whole house was. My mum inherited it when Grandma died. Look at these . . .' she leads me over to the bed. There's a battered old trunk lying open on the quilt, with clothes spilling out of it. 'I found them in the loft,' Holly says, her eyes gleaming with excitement. 'They must have been my great-grandmother's to be this old! I'm going to wear this one to the dance. What do you think?' She smoothes down the dress she's wearing.

I look at her and smile. 'It's beautiful.'

'You can wear one too – if you like.' She looks at me hopefully. 'I thought this one would go really well with your eyes, although I haven't quite worked out what colour they are are yet. They seem to be different every day.' She holds up one of the dresses. It's the same style as hers but in peacock blue with a silver fringe of beads.

'Please say you'll wear it – we'll look so cool!'

I take the dress from her. It's stunning. So much nicer than the black dress I'd brought. 'I'll wear it.'

Holly whoops.

Once I've changed we go back downstairs, dancing all the way.

Holly's bedroom is in the basement and, unlike the rest of the rooms I've seen with their high ceilings and antique furniture, it's really cosy and snug. The walls are lined with bookshelves and there are teetering piles of books all over the carpet.

Holly goes straight over to a laptop on her desk. 'This is the video I was telling you about – the one that teaches you the Charleston.' She presses play and beckons me over. 'Come on – it's so much fun.'

After a few tries we don't need the video any more and soon we're dancing back up into the hallway. With the chequered floor and chandelier it's easy to pretend that we've gone back in time to the 1920s. I'm not sure how long we dance for but I love every second of it.

Finally, we crash down on to the bottom step of the main staircase, giggling and out of breath.

'Where's your au pair?' I ask, wondering what Svetlana must think of the noise we're making.

'Oh, she's in starring in the pantomime at the Town Hall. She's one of the Ugly Sisters. It's her dream role.' Holly grins at me. 'I'm so glad you've moved to Fairhollow. I mean, I'm not glad that you had to move away from your dad, and I know it hasn't been the best week for you, but it's so much more fun with you here.' She looks down into her lap, suddenly sad. 'I didn't think I'd be able to go to the dance this year.'

'Why not?'

'Oh, just certain people being a pain.'

'Izzy and Vivien?'

Holly nods. 'I'd realised that the best way to keep them off my back was to try and make myself invisible. But now you're here, I don't have to do that any more. I can get back to having fun again.'

I look at her. 'Is that why you're always reading in school? To try and make yourself invisible?'

Holly nods. 'I love books so it's not a problem, but it is good to be able to have conversations too.'

I frown. Holly's so much fun that I can't imagine why she's so unpopular. 'Why do they pick on you?'

Holly shrugs. 'I don't know.' She looks away, like she's embarrassed. 'So, did you get your playlist done for the dance?'

I feel a sudden stab of panic. 'Yes, but would it be OK if I just give it one last check before we leave? I keep having this nightmare where I give it to Mr G and there's nothing on it.'

Holly leaps to her feet. 'Of course. Come on.'

We go back down to her bedroom and I take

my iPod from my bag. As soon as I switch it on, I see the battery icon on the screen is empty.

'Oh no!' I clap my hand to my mouth.

'What's up?'

'I forgot to bring my charger and my battery's dead.'

Holly grins. 'Don't worry. I've got one. Pass it to me.'

Just as I hand it to her there's a loud rap on the front door.

'It must be the taxi,' Holly says. 'I ordered one earlier.'

'But my iPod . . .'

Holly looks down at it. 'Oh – er – it's OK now, look.' She hands it back looking really flustered. The battery icon on the screen is now full.

'But how –?'

'Come on, we need to go.' Holly rushes past me, her cheeks bright red.

10

Apart from the teachers and a couple of Year Nines who've been roped in to check tickets and serve drinks, we're the very first people to arrive at the dance.

It's like the hall's had one of those TV-show makeovers. All the chairs have been taken out and the walls are draped in strings of gold and red tinsel. A huge Christmas tree is standing in the middle of the stage and garlands of holly and sprigs of mistletoe are hanging down from the ceiling. I've had such a lovely afternoon with Holly that for the first time since arriving in Fairhollow, I actually feel festive. Mr Graham calls me over to the music system at the side of the stage. I take my iPod from my bag and check the battery – it's still full.

'Here's my playlist,' I say, handing it over.

'Excellent,' he says with a grin. 'For someone with your musical ear, I'm expecting very good things.'

'Thank you, sir.'

Grinning, I head back to Holly. As the first track on my list starts playing over the speakers, she grabs my hands.

'Shall we do the Charleston while we wait?' She gestures around the empty hall. 'Look how much space we've got.'

I nod and follow her over to the centre of the hall. Soon we're laughing and dancing like we were in her house. It feels so weird and so, so good to be having this much fun at Fairhollow High. It's like it's cancelling out all of the bad stuff that's happened here this week. And then I hear a loud cough, and Holly's face falls.

I turn to see Izzy, Vivien and Stephen standing

right behind us. Some other students are filing into the hall behind them.

'What a couple of weirdos,' Izzy says loudly, shaking her head.

Vivien nods in agreement. 'I know.'

'They must think they look cool dancing on their own.' Stephen sneers.

Izzy narrows her eyes at us. 'Do you? Because it isn't cool at all. You just look really sad.'

It's like I've been struck by a red-hot bolt of anger. I hate Izzy. I hate her more than I've hated anyone in my life before. I can't stand having her anywhere near me. I wish she'd just disappear. Izzy smirks at me – and topples over backwards on to the floor.

'Ow!' she cries, scrambling to get back up.

My anger and hatred instantly disappear and my head starts thumping. I push past the others, ignoring their stares, and head out into the corridor. Loads of students are arriving now, all looking immaculate in their fancy outfits, the total opposite to how I feel. I rush out of a nearby fire exit and sit on the steps. I take a deep breath. And another. What just happened? What keeps happening? I've never hated anyone as much as I hated Izzy just then. Why are my emotions going so crazy all of the time? After a couple of minutes I start getting really cold. So, making a mental note to avoid Izzy and the others, I go back inside. When I get back, the hall's full of students and I can tell immediately that something's wrong. They're way too quiet and they're all looking in exactly the same direction. I follow their gaze to the centre of the hall, where Holly and Izzy are squaring up to one another like they're about to have a fight. I start barging my way through the crowd towards them, my heart pounding. But I'm too late. Before I can get there, Izzy prods Holly in the shoulder and Holly pushes her back. Then the lights flicker and there's a loud bang, followed by the tinkling sound of breaking glass echoing all around the hall. There's a stunned silence as everyone gazes around in shock. Every light in the ceiling has blown. Even the fairy lights on the Christmas tree have gone out. We're plunged into darkness, and people start to panic. Mr Graham's voice comes over the speakers, asking us calmly to leave the hall. I head over to Holly, picking my way through the broken glass.

Like everyone else, she's looking really shocked. But unlike everyone else, I'm sure I can see a slight smile on her lips.

'Holly, are you OK?' I say as I reach her. 'What happened?'

'I'm fine,' she says and she grips on to my arm. 'No, scrap that – I'm brilliant.'

'Are you sure?'

She nods at me in the darkness. 'Come on, let's go.'

Due to the 'unforseen power surge', as Mr Graham puts it, the dance is called off. The other students hang around in groups outside but Holly seems really keen to go and, not wanting to bump into

Izzy in case she makes me go crazy again, I'm definitely not going to argue with her.

'Let's go back to mine,' she says, linking arms with me and putting her head down against the cold. 'Svetlana will still be at the panto and your aunt won't be expecting you back for ages.'

'Sure,' I say, 'let's face it – it was far more fun at yours than it was at the dance!'

Holly laughs, but then we both fall silent. I can't stop thinking about what made the lights blow out like that.

As we walk past the entrance to the park I see the lamppost that blew when Holly leant against it on Monday and a shiver runs up my spine. It has to be a coincidence. Maybe the power supply in Fairhollow is erratic; everything does seem pretty ancient here. But then I think of my iPod. The battery icon was definitely empty when I handed it to Holly. And yet when she handed it back it was fully charged. Is it Fairhollow that's causing these freaky things to happen – or is it Holly? We carry on walking in silence but in my head, the unanswered questions are getting louder and louder.

When we get back to Holly's she takes me straight to the kitchen for hot chocolate. I sit down at the huge pine table and she starts heating some milk on the stove. My head is so full of questions now I decide to say one out loud.

'Did you . . . ?' But I break off. How can I ask her if she made the lights blow? It would sound really nuts.

'What?' Holly says, still stirring the milk.

'Do you have . . . ?'

Holly turns round smiling. 'Chocolate sprinkles to go on top? Yes, definitely.'

'No. I wasn't talking about the drink.' I look down at my lap. 'Do you have some kind of connection with electricity?'

'What – what do you mean?' Holly's voice is so filled with dread I have to look at her. Her face has drained of colour and her smile has totally disappeared. She looks as if she's seen a ghost.

'Like, around electrical appliances.' My face flushes. 'Sorry, I know it sounds crazy, it's just that there was that weird thing that happened with the lamppost and when I gave you my iPod the battery recharged and then tonight . . . I was just wondering if, I don't know, you had some kind of super-charged energy field or something.' As soon as I say it I feel ridiculous. What even is a super-charged energy field?! I grimace. 'I'm sorry. I'm just being stupid. Forget I said anything.'

But Holly remains motionless at the stove, with the spoon in her hand.

I'm hit by a wave of anxiety so strong I have to close my eyes and take a deep breath. When I open them again, Holly has put taken the pan from the stove and she's standing right in front of me.

'I – er – there's something I have to tell you,' she says, looking ultra-serious. 'But you have to promise me you won't freak out, and you won't tell anyone else.'

'Of course.' As soon as the words leave my

mouth I feel a wave of relief.

'I really mean it,' she says, looking me right in the eyes. 'You have to promise.'

'I promise,' I say.

Holly sits down beside me. 'I'm not . . .' she looks away. 'I'm not like other girls.'

'What do you mean?'

'I mean, I do have powers – a power.'

'Around electricity?'

Holly nods. 'But it's not just that.'

I look at her questioningly and anxiety starts bubbling in my stomach again.

'I . . .' she lowers her voice to a whisper . . . 'I'm a witch.'

I burst out laughing.

'Ha, ha! Very funny. You do realise Halloween was two months ago?'

But Holly isn't laughing. She isn't even smiling. Her eyes are all glassy with tears.

'Holly?'

A tear spills down on to her face.

I reach out and grab her hand. 'Holly, what do you mean you're a witch?'

'Exactly that,' she says, glumly.

'What, as in, making spells and riding around on a broomstick?' My brain can't take this all in. How can she be a witch? Witches don't even exist. This has to be a prank. But why would Holly prank me over something like this? It doesn't make any sense. And she can't be tricking me. She looks way too upset. Now she's actually crying.

'I only found out about it a couple of months ago,' she says, wiping her tears with the back of her hand, 'when my power started.'

I'm about to tell her that what she's saying is crazy but then I look at her and I'm overcome with the strongest sense that what she's saying is the truth. I fumble in my bag for a tissue and pass it to her. 'The thing with electricity?'

She nods and wipes away her tears. 'Yes. I'm an energy harnesser.' She gives an embarrassed laugh. 'I'm just not so good at the harnessing bit yet.'

'But I don't understand . . .'

Holly pulls her chair up closer. 'Don't freak out. But the truth is that there have always been witches in Fairhollow since, like, forever. Hundreds of years ago, there were loads of them, but now there's only a few.'

Everything Holly is saying to me, every single word that's coming from her mouth, is completely nuts, and yet I can't shake the absolute feeling of certainty that she's being genuine; that she's telling the truth. 'So, you're one of the few?'

'Yes.' She gives a sarcastic laugh. 'I won the witch lottery, woohoo! There are some bonuses though, I guess. I never need chargers.'

I sit in silence for a moment, trying to make sense of what she's just said. 'So, are all witches energy harnessers?'

Holly shakes her head. 'No. Every witch has one special power, but there are different things that power can be. I don't know them all but I do know that some of them can be healers, and some . . . some can be empaths.' She looks at me pointedly when she says that, like she's trying to tell me something.

'What's an empath?'

'It's someone who can read another person's emotions.' She's still looking at me like she's trying to tell me something.

My mouth goes dry. 'What do you mean, *read another person's emotions*?'

'Well, if a person is feeling angry or sad, an empath will pick up on it.'

'What, like, feel that emotion too?'

Holly nods.

I think of the way my emotions have been swinging all over the place since I've got here and start to shiver. 'But I've just been really stressed,' I mutter.

'What?'

'Nothing. I . . .' A chill fills my body like a freezing fog.

'Sometimes they're able to get visions too,'

Holly says, cautiously. 'If a person has been through something really traumatic, an empath might see that thing. Like a flashback.'

A flashback? Instantly I think of what I saw when I was with Vivien. The man in the car and the crying girl. Could that have been – Vivien's past? I stare at Holly. 'What are you trying to say? Do you think – do you think I'm an empath?'

Holly looks at me and nods 'I can sense it in you. I've been sensing it for a few days now. That day when you were sick in the toilet and when you told me about the vision. But I didn't know how to . . .' she breaks off.

'How to tell me I am a witch?'

Holly looks down and nods.

My head is spinning. This whole thing feels like a weird dream, but the weirdest thing about it is that I know that it isn't. I'm wide awake and so is Holly, and everything that has happened, everything that has been said, is real.

'I have to go,' I say, getting to my feet.

Holly looks at me, her eyes wide with concern. 'Are you OK?'

I nod, even though I feel about as far from OK as it's physically possible to be.

'I just need to be on my own for a bit. It's a lot to take in.'

Holly nods. 'I know. Call me tomorrow. Please?'

I nod. And then I stumble my way over to the door.

After a terrible night's sleep I wake up the next morning to the sound of the text alert going off on my phone. I grab it hoping it's Holly telling me that last night was all some kind of crazy joke. But the message is from Ellie.

How you doing BFF?! Do you want to Skype? 😊 **xxxx**

I stare at the phone and mentally compose a reply: *Oh, I'm doing just great, considering I found out last night that I might be a witch!!!* It sounds so crazy I want to laugh. But I can't because for some stupid reason I still have the feeling that Holly was telling me the truth. And surely that only backs up what she was saying: I was reading her emotions because I'm an empath. And I'm an empath because I'm a witch. I click Ellie's message shut. I can't Skype with her. I can't do anything until I've seen Holly. I quickly send her a text.

Can we meet?

Holly texts straight back, like she was waiting to hear from me.

Yes of course. When? Where? Hx

By the crossroads. 15 mins xoxo

I get out of bed and pull on a hoodie and a pair of jeans. Downstairs, I can hear Aunt Clara moving about in the kitchen, getting ready for another Sunday opening. I quickly wash my face and clean my teeth and head down. Aunt Clara is standing by the toaster, holding a plate and knife.

'You're up bright and early,' she says as soon as she sees me.

'Yes, I just need to pop out for a bit.'

Aunt Clara looks at the clock. 'At this time? What for?'

'I'm doing a bit of Christmas shopping with Eve. I said I'd go round to her house first.' I try to stop my face from flushing and fail. I turn and pretend to fiddle with one of my boots.

'Oh.' Aunt Clara sounds really disappointed.

My heart starts to pound. Has she realised I'm lying?

'I was going to ask if you fancied earning yourself a bit of extra pocket money in the shop today,' Aunt Clara continues and I breathe a sigh of relief. 'I'm expecting it to be really busy with it being the last weekend before Christmas.'

'I can do later on,' I offer, heading for the door. 'I won't be long.'

'What about breakfast?'

'I'll get something when I'm out.'

When I get on to the High Street the only other signs of life are a couple of shop owners unlocking their stores. The sky is chalk white. I half-walk, half-jog up to the crossroads. Holly is waiting for me there, holding two takeaway cups.

'Hot chocolate?' she says, holding one out to me. 'I got some from The Cup and Saucer, since we didn't get to have any last night.' She gives me an apologetic smile.

I take the drink and wrap my hands around it to soak up the warmth. I look at her for a second, waiting for her to say that last night was all an elaborate joke, but she doesn't. She just looks down at the ground like she's embarrassed or sad. Or both.

'Where do you want to go?' she finally asks, quietly.

I sigh. To have this conversation we need to be somewhere quiet, somewhere no one will overhear us, and somewhere I'll feel safe. I instantly think of the old oak tree. 'Follow me.'

I lead Holly across the High Street and up to the footpath into the woods. The ground is frozen solid and the fallen leaves are all glimmering with frost. As soon as I see the tree I feel a little bit better. 'I found this place after my first day at Fairhollow High,' I explain as I lead Holly over to the nook between the roots and we sit down. I look down at my hot chocolate. 'Last night wasn't a prank, was it?'

'No.' Holly says quietly.

'Can you tell me some more – you know, about being a . . .' I can't even bring myself to say it, it sounds so crazy.

'Sure. Though I don't know loads, to be honest. Like I said, I only really found out myself a couple of months ago.'

'How?'

'Well, first of all, I kept getting really bad static whenever I touched something electrical, and if I tried to change channels on the TV it would switch itself off – that was really annoying! And then I blew up the coffee-maker – it started spraying out all over the place.' She laughs. 'It did look kind of cool – like a coffee volcano erupting – but Mum didn't see the funny side when she came in. It even got on the ceiling!'

'But why did you think that made you a witch?'

'Because of my grandma.'

I look at her questioningly.

'When I was little me and my grandma were really close. She looked after me whenever my parents were away. She used to say things to me – things that didn't quite make sense at the time.'

'Like what?'

'Like, "you and I aren't like other people, Holly, one day you'll understand." Whenever I asked her what she meant she said she'd tell me properly on my thirteenth birthday.' Holly looks down at her lap, sadly. 'But she never got the chance. She died when I was twelve.'

'But how does that mean you're a witch? She could have been talking about something totally different, like – like, your personalities or something.'

Holly shakes her head. 'No, there was definitely more to it than that. She used to tell me stories about the witches of Fairhollow all the time when I was little. That's all I thought they were – stories – but now I know she was trying to prepare me. I should have listened to her more. She talked about all these different powers, but I can't remember most of them now. I do know about empaths, though, and I'm pretty sure that my grandma was a weathercaster.'

'A weathercaster? What does that mean?'

'It's a witch who's able to control the weather. One time, when it was raining really hard on my birthday, she said this little poem thing and the sun suddenly came out, like, within a second.'

'Seriously?'

'Yep.' Holly looks gloomy. 'I wish I'd got

that power instead of the blowing-up-appliances one. Although knowing my luck, if I had been a weathercaster I'd probably make hurricanes happen all the time.'

I suddenly feel really sad. As sad as Holly looks; as if her unhappiness is soaking into the ground around her and coming up inside of me. So this is what being an empath is.

I shuffle closer to her. 'Can you try thinking of something that makes you feel really happy?'

Holly scrunches up her forehead. 'OK.' She closes her eyes and slowly a smile spreads across her face.

I'm filled with a warm glow of happiness. It feels as if the sun's burst out of the clouds above us. 'I can feel it,' I whisper.

Holly opens her eyes and stares at me. 'Really?'

'What were you thinking about?'

'All the books I'm going to get for Christmas.'

We both laugh.

'Let's try again,' Holly says, looking way

happier now. 'But this time, I won't tell you what emotion I'm feeling.'

'OK.'

We both close our eyes. For a few moments I feel nothing. Then I feel a creeping sensation of dread coming up through my body. I quickly open my eyes. 'Oh, that was horrible.'

Holly looks at me excitedly. 'What did you get?'

'It was like I was really dreading something. What were you thinking about?'

Holly grins. 'My physics homework.'

We both laugh and I feel a tiny glimmer of hope. Maybe this being-an-empath thing won't be so bad after all. At least now I know what's been causing my weird mood swings. Maybe I'll be able to find a way to control them. But then I'm struck by another question.

'But why do I have this power?'

Holly looks at me, all serious. 'Your mum.'

'Yes, but . . .'

'It's a hereditary thing.'

'Are you saying my mum was a witch?'

Holly shakes her head. 'Not necessarily. Mine isn't. She thinks the whole "witches of Fairhollow" thing is just folklore. But your grandma could have been one – or your great-grandma.'

My grandma died before I was born. I imagine sitting down for dinner with Aunt Clara and saying, 'Hey, was your mum a witch?' I can't help smiling.

'What's funny?'

'This – it's all so crazy.'

Holly sighs. 'Tell me about it.'

'So, me moving to Fairhollow triggered my powers?'

Holly nods. 'I think so.'

'So what are we supposed to do now? I mean, it's not as if we can tell anyone, is it? We can hardly start up a Facebook group.'

I laugh but Holly looks deadly serious. 'We have to choose.'

'Choose what?'

'Choose whether we want to be a Silver Witch

or a Blood Witch.'

I frown at her. 'What's the difference?'

'Silver Witches use their powers to help people and do good.'

'And Blood Witches?'

'Blood Witches are terrible.' Holly shudders and I feel a rush of dread way more powerful than when she was thinking about her physics homework. I pull my coat tighter around me. Holly looks at me with wide eyes. 'Seriously, they're so vile there's no way I'd ever join them.'

'But how do you know what they're like? It's not as if you've actually met any.' I look at her. 'Have you?'

Holly nods. 'Oh yes.'

The feeling of dread inside me grows and then I have a horrible realisation. 'Have I – have I met them too?'

Holly nods.

'Izzy and Vivien?'

'Yes. And Stephen.'

Now I'm certain I'm not just feeling Holly's dread – I'm feeling my own too.

'They tried to get me to join them, but I refused.' Holly says. 'There's no way I could use my powers to hurt people like they do.'

'Me neither.'

We look at each other.

'So you'll be a Silver Witch too?'

'Yes. Of course.'

Holly links her arm through mine. 'Oh, I'm so glad you're here now. It was so horrible before, being the only one.'

'It must have been.' I look at her. 'But how do you know you're the only Silver? Surely there have to be others here.'

'There must be, but I've never sensed them – not until you came.'

We sit in silence for a moment. Then my phone chimes with a text. It's from Aunt Clara.

Dawn has called in sick. Please can you

**come and help in the shop asap? Thank
you, Aunt Clara**

I clamber to my feet. 'I'm really sorry, I've got
to go.'

Holly frowns. 'Why?'

'My aunt wants me to help her in the shop.'

Holly stands up and looks at me, concerned.
'Wait, are you OK about all this?'

'Yes. Kind of. I think. It's so much to take in,
but I'm really glad I've got you to talk to about it.'

'Me too.' Holly hugs me. 'I can't believe I'm not
going to see you now till after Christmas.'

I look at her in shock. 'Your holiday!' In all the
drama of the last twenty-four hours, I've totally
forgotten that Holly's going away with her parents
for Christmas. 'When do you get back?'

Holly sighs. 'New Year's Eve. This is going to
be the longest Christmas ever.'

'Tell me about it.'

'Just call or text me if you need to chat. I know

when I first realised I freaked out.'

I nod. 'Will do.' I look up at the oak tree. Its huge branches stir slightly, like it's waving at me.

Holly takes hold of both my hands. 'Silver forever?'

I nod. 'Silver forever.' A jolt runs up my spine. It's the same feeling I got when I confronted Izzy and the others outside Gym; a feeling of real power. And even though I should be really messed up by all of this I suddenly feel really good. I look at Holly and smile.

Paper Soul is packed when I get back. People are swarming around the bookshelves and every table in the café is full. Aunt Clara is behind the counter looking super-stressed.

'Nessa!' she cries as soon as she sees me. 'Thanks so much for coming back. I hope Eve didn't mind.'

'What? Oh, no, she was fine.' I slip behind the counter to join her.

'I'm so sorry to do this to you,' Aunt Clara says. 'But I do have some good news. Your friend, Ellie, rang while you were out. She wanted to know if she could come and visit.'

I stare at her in shock. 'What did you say?'

Aunt Clara smiles. 'I said of course. She's more than welcome.'

I feel a burst of happiness but it's tinged with worry. How can I ever tell Ellie what's happened since I got here? She'll think I'd gone crazy.

'Is that OK?' Aunt Clara says, looking concerned. I guess she must have noticed my frown.

'Yes, yes of course. It's great. When's she coming?'

'New Year's Eve.' Aunt Clara starts ringing up a customer's bill on the till. 'So she'll be able to come to the Paper Soul party.'

I look at her in surprise. 'You're having a New Year's Eve party?'

'Yes. I have one every year.'

I'm surprised. Aunt Clara seems way too uptight

to be the party type. But maybe she's just uptight when I'm around. Aunt Clara gives me one of her X-ray stares and I quickly rearrange my face into a smile. 'That sounds really cool.'

Aunt Clara sends me over to tidy up the bookshelves. While I'm in the Astrology section I have a brainwave. Maybe Paper Soul has a section on witches. Maybe a book will help answer the questions that keep popping into my head. I weave in and out of the customers, searching. But there's nothing. I'm about to give up when a customer asks me if I can get a book down from the top shelf for her. I fetch the mini-step ladder and reach up for the book. As I'm up there I spot a small handwritten sign on the next shelf along, saying *WITCHCRAFT*.

I hand the customer her book then look back at the shelf, feeling a buzz of excitement.

'Nessa!' Aunt Clara calls to me across the murmur of the shop.

Pretending I haven't heard her, I start scanning

the titles. *Healing Spells, Wiccan Rituals, The History of Witchcraft.*

'Nessa!' Aunt Clara calls again, so sharply the chatter from the café fades.

I sigh and turn to look at her.

'Can you come here please?' she calls.

I come down from the step ladder and walk over to the counter.

'What's up?'

'I need you to help me out on the till.'

As I stand next to Aunt Clara my insides start crawling with anxiety, but I know it can't be mine. I have nothing to be anxious about. I watch her counting out change and the feeling grows. It must be Aunt Clara – but what is she so worried about?

'Are you sure you're OK?'

Dad asks me this every time we talk on the phone, and every time I say the same thing.

'Yes, Dad, honestly, I'm fine.' I sit back in my chair behind the shop counter and take a sip of my ginger tea. Aunt Clara was up really late last night, making food for the New Year's Eve party, so I've opened the shop this morning to give her a lie-in. It seems as if all of Fairhollow is having a lie-in too – I haven't had a single customer.

'I'm really sorry I wasn't able to get any time off work over the Christmas break,' Dad says, his voice faint and slightly muffled.

'It's fine,' I say, and I'm only half-lying. It's actually been quite good having a bit of time on my own this Christmas to get my head around everything that's happened. And one thing's for certain – there's no way I could ever tell Dad.

'So, you had a good time with Aunt Clara?' Dad asks, for about the third time this conversation and the tenth time since Christmas Day.

'Yes, it was great.' And again, I'm not really lying. Christmas with Aunt Clara was about as different from a traditional Christmas as possible. There was no big family get-together, no carol singing and obviously no turkey. But it was OK. I'm used to it being just Dad and me at Christmas anyway, and actually the dinner was quite nice. Aunt Clara made a nut roast with marmite gravy, which wasn't nearly as gross as it sounds, and roast potatoes. And we had a vegan Christmas pudding. After the shock of the beetroot brownies, I didn't dare ask what was in it, but it tasted really good. And having a few days just the two of us seems to have really helped Aunt Clara relax around me.

'That's great,' Dad says. 'So when's Ellie arriving?'

I look at the clock on the café wall. 'Any time now. It's so exciting!'

Dad laughs. 'Your Aunt Clara won't know what's hit her. The giggling! The noise!'

'I don't know what you mean,' I say in a pretend-cross voice.

Just then, the bell above the shop door jangles. I look up but there's no one there. 'I'd better go, Dad, I think I've got a customer.'

'OK, love, well, happy New Year's Eve. Have a great time with Ellie.'

'Thanks, Dad. Love you.'

'Love you too.'

I slip out from behind the counter and walk through the café into the shop. I check each of the alcoves of books but they're all deserted.

'Hello?' I say.

There's no reply. Maybe someone came in and went straight out again. They must have moved really quickly for me not to have seen them. I'm about to head back to the counter when I notice something on the floor by the door. Something black. My heart starts pounding. Surely it's not what I think it is. But it is. A dead blackbird is lying on the mat, its long orange beak pointing up into the air. My skin breaks out into a cold sweat. Someone must have put it there. But who? And why? There's a piece of paper beside the bird. I crouch down and pick it up, my stomach churning.

'*Happy New Year, Nessa!*' someone has scrawled in red ink. There's something familiar about the large loop of the letter Y. I remember the note on my locker. Izzy! But how had she put the bird there without me seeing? I sit back on my heels feeling sick with dread. The past few days with Aunt Clara have been like being in a bubble. They gave me the chance to push all the horrible things that have happened to the back of my mind. But now that bubble has been well and truly burst. I feel a surge of panic. I can't let Aunt Clara see the bird. I have to get rid of it. I race back behind the counter to get a bag, which I put over my hand like a giant glove. But just as I get back to the bird and start to scoop it up, the bell jangles again and the shop door bursts open. I bite down on my lip to stop myself screaming.

'Nessa!'

I drop the bird and jump to my feet. Ellie's standing in the doorway, grinning at me like crazy.

'I can't believe I'm actually here!' she cries. 'It's so good to see you. I've missed you so much! Oh my God – what is that?'

I follow Ellie's gaze down to the floor. The bird's spindly feet are poking out of the bag.

I quickly crouch down and scoop it up. 'It's – someone just put it there. I was trying to clear it up.'

Ellie crouches down and stares at me, horrified. 'What? But who?' She looks down at the note. 'What does that mean, Nessa?' Ellie's grey eyes grow wide with concern .'Why would someone do something like this?'

'I've been having a few problems with a couple of bullies in my class.' I scrunch the note up and stuff it in the bag with the bird.

Ellie shakes her head in disbelief. 'That is beyond bullying. That is – sick.'

'I know.' I tie a knot in the top of the bag and pull it as tight as I can.

'Have you told your aunt?' Ellie asks as we both stand up.

I shake my head. 'No. It's OK, I can handle it.'

'Oh, Nessa. You should have told me.' Ellie's eyes fill with tears and I feel a wave of sorrow coming from her.

'Honestly, I'm fine,' I smile at her weakly.

Ellie frowns. 'You shouldn't have to put up with it.' She looks at me for a moment, then grabs me in a hug. Her hair smells of her usual coconut shampoo, and it reminds me of sleepovers and going swimming together – a time when everything was happy and nice. I blink tears away. Those days are gone, at least for now, and I have to stay strong.

'Things aren't that bad, honestly,' I say. 'I've made a really good friend. Holly, you know, the one I told you about?'

Ellie nods. Then she looks down at the bag. 'What are you going to do with it?' she says, lowering her voice to a whisper.

'I don't know.' We both look at each other and it's just like the time we got caught sending notes to each other in Maths and had to go to the Head's office. Even though it feels massively inappropriate, I get the horrible urge to laugh. Ellie's obviously feeling the same because she's biting her bottom lip the way she always does when she's trying not to giggle. 'I'm sorry,' she gasps, 'I know it isn't funny, but . . .'

And that's all it takes to set me off. 'Welcome to my new life, Ells,' I say, gesturing down at the bag. 'The wonderful town of Fairhollow, where people send you dead blackbirds as a New Year's gift.'

We cling on to each other, laughing. 'I am so glad to see you!' I say.

'I bet,' she replies, looking pointedly at the bag, which sets us both off again.

'Well, hello, you must be Ellie.' We both jump at the sound of Aunt Clara's voice. She's standing behind the counter, smiling at us. I quickly kick the bag behind Ellie's suitcase.

'Yes. Aunt Clara, this is Ellie. Ellie, this is my Aunt Clara.'

'Hello,' Ellie calls out.

'Lovely to meet you,' Aunt Clara says. 'And lovely to see Nessa looking so happy.' She smiles at me and I feel warm waves of relief pouring down the shop from her. 'You must have really missed each other.'

We both nod.

'Why don't you take Ellie's things up to your room, Nessa, then take her out and show her round town?'

'Are you sure you don't need any help in the shop?'

Aunt Clara shakes her head. 'I'll be fine. Dawn'll be here soon, to help me set up for the party.'

Just then, my phone chimes with a text. It's a message from Holly.

Hey! I'm back! Want to go sledging? Hxx

Aunt Clara and Ellie look at me expectantly.

'It's Eve,' I say, my cheeks flushing.

'Eve?' Ellie looks at me questioningly.

My cheeks flush even redder. Obviously I've never mentioned Eve's name to Ellie before. 'Yes, she's a friend I've made up here.'

Ellie looks puzzled. 'Oh. But I thought –'

'She wants to know if we can go sledging,' I interrupt, praying Ellie doesn't mention Holly's name in front of Aunt Clara.

'Ooh, that would be awesome,' Ellie cries.

'You can borrow my old sledge,' Aunt Clara says with a grin. 'I'll go and get it from the storeroom.'

I breathe a huge sigh of relief and make a mental note to tell Ellie about Aunt Clara's weird issue with Holly as soon as I can.

Once we've got Ellie's case upstairs, Aunt Clara finds us her old sled and makes us a flask of ginger tea. I somehow manage to keep the carrier bag with the bird hidden until we're out of the door.

'What are you going to do with it?' Ellie says as we trudge up the High Street. There's been a fresh snowfall in the night and the whole place is covered in a blanket of white which sparkles gold in the sunshine.

'Bury it, I guess.'

I decide to bury the bird up by the old oak tree. I don't want to think about how it died, but at least I can give it a peaceful resting place.

I pick a spot a few yards from the tree and try to start digging with a spoon I slipped into my pocket in the café – but the ground is frozen. I feel a stab of panic and glance across at Ellie, trying to pick up if she's having any negative feelings, but all I get is a strange mixture of happiness and concern.

She smiles at me. 'It's so good to see you again, Ness.'

I smile back, trying not to think how weird all of this is. 'You too.'

'And I'm so glad you've got Eve and Holly —' she pulls her woolly hat down tighter over her blonde curls — 'even though it makes me feel a bit sad thinking of you having other friends.'

I look down. 'I feel a bit sad too — thinking about you with Helen.'

'Do you?'

I nod. 'Actually, there's something I need to tell you. It's a bit embarrassing but hey, I'm trying and failing to bury a dead bird right now, so I have no shame!' I take a deep breath and look up at Ellie again. 'I only have one new friend. It was Holly who texted before, but I had to pretend it was Eve because Aunt Clara doesn't like Holly.'

Ellie frowns. 'What? Why not?'

'Because she thinks Holly's trouble. But she isn't, honestly. You'll really like her.'

Ellie smiles and shakes her head. 'Wow, things certainly haven't been dull for you since you got here.'

I laugh. 'That's for sure!'

Ellie crouches down next to me as I give up on the ground and just scoop out some snow from a nearby drift. I gently place the bird into the hole and cover it up again. 'I have to say, when I was imagining coming up here and all the things we'd do together, I never, for one second, thought we'd be having a funeral for a bird.'

We look at each other and laugh.

I look back at the bird. 'Do you think we should say something?'

'Yes,' Ellie says softly.

I say the first thing that comes into my head. 'Goodbye. I hope you'll be peaceful here.'

'Yes,' Ellie says. 'Rest in peace, little bird.'

I swallow hard to stop myself from crying. 'Ells?'

'Yes?'

'I'm so glad you're here.'

Ellie reaches for my hand and holds it tightly. 'Me too.'

13

Two things surprise me about Aunt Clara's New Year's Eve party. First, and most obviously, the fact that she's having a party at all, and second, that so many people have come to it. By eleven o'clock, every alcove in the bookshop is crammed with people chatting and laughing and drinking mulled wine. It feels as if the whole town has turned up; the whole town apart from Holly. When Holly met me and Ellie earlier to go sledging I invited her, even though there's no way Aunt Clara would have approved. It just felt too cruel not to. She said no, but I could tell by the way she said it, and the feeling of awkwardness that came washing over me that she was just making an excuse. It made me realise that she must know how Aunt Clara feels about her after all, and that made me feel even more horrible.

I look over at Aunt Clara. She's laughing and joking with one of the musicians from the band that are playing tonight. She's wearing an emerald-green dress that goes brilliantly with her flame-red hair and she looks happier and more relaxed than I've ever seen her. I get a sinking feeling. It must have been me who made her so uptight before. I bet she was having parties every night of the week before I moved in.

Ellie comes over, holding two glasses of fruit punch. She hands one to me and smiles.

Ever since Ellie got here this morning, I've been running through imaginary conversations in my head. *'Guess what, Ellie? I've discovered I'm a witch. Yes, that's right, witch as in broomstick. And that's not all – it turns out I've got this secret power. I can tell how people are feeling. Oh yes, and you know the school bullies who sent me the dead bird? Well, they're witches too! Bad ones.'*

I sigh. How can I possibly tell her? She'll think I've gone totally bonkers.

'Have you seen the fiddle player in the band?' Ellie opens her eyes wide. 'Seriously cute with a capital C!'

I glance over to the café area where the band are setting up. The boy with the fiddle doesn't look much older than us. He's got wavy black hair and he's wearing black boots, faded jeans and a plaid shirt. Ellie's right, even from this distance I can tell he's cute.

Aunt Clara clinks a knife against a glass and we all fall silent. 'I just wanted to thank everyone so much for coming tonight,' she says, smiling around the shop. 'It's lovely to see you all and I hope you're having a great time. Now, I have a very special treat for you. The folk band, Blue Harbour, will be playing some songs for us until the countdown to midnight.' Aunt Clara raises her glass to the band and everyone claps and cheers. I feel a sudden burst of pride. It's so nice being part of all this.

As the band start playing, I make my way through the café to the toilet. Today has been good, in spite of its horrible start. Seeing Ellie in Fairhollow has made me realise that she isn't as far away as I'd thought. It's reassured me that our friendship can last the year. Aunt Clara seems way more chilled, and Holly is back from holiday. Things aren't so bad after all.

When I get back into the café, the fiddle player's playing a solo. His bow arm's moving so fast it's practically blurring. I stop and watch him, mesmerised. His arm is tanned and muscular and there's a black leather friendship bracelet on his wrist. I love how the other musicians are so in tune with him, watching his every move, as they play along quietly in the background. It makes me want to go and get my guitar and join them. The solo comes to an end and the others start playing louder. The boy catches me looking at him and smiles. My face instantly flushes. I quickly turn to head back to Ellie. But what I see makes my blood freeze. She's been surrounded by Izzy, Vivien and Stephen. I see Izzy throw back her head and give a tinkly laugh. I stride over to them, barging past people on the way. But I don't care. I have to get to Ellie. I have to keep them away from Ellie.

'Oh, hey, Nessa,' Izzy says as soon as I reach them. 'We were just chatting to your *adorable* friend from London.'

'That's great,' I say through gritted teeth. 'Ellie, could you do me a favour, please? Could you pop upstairs and get my guitar from the bedroom? Aunt Clara's asked me to sort something out in the shop.'

'Sure.' Ellie glances at Izzy and the others uncertainly and heads upstairs.

'What are you doing?' I hiss at Izzy as soon as Ellie's gone.

'Just being friendly,' Izzy says. She's wearing heavy black eyeliner and bright red lipstick. She looks like a really evil china doll. 'We like being friendly, don't we?' she turns to Vivien and Stephen, who nod and smirk.

'Yes, we do,' says Vivien. 'Did you get our little gift this morning?'

'Yes, I got it.'

Izzy's smile vanishes and she moves in close so she can whisper in my ear. 'That gift was a warning. We want you out of Fairhollow – for good.'

'Oh, really?' I say loudly, standing my ground.

'Yes, really,' Izzy snarls. 'You're not welcome here.'

The other two draw closer but I'm not intimidated. Just like before at the school dance, I feel strangely powerful. It's as if I have roots going right down into the ground, like the old oak tree, keeping me strong.

'I'm not going anywhere,' I hiss back at them. 'You don't frighten me.'

Izzy stares at me, her eyes icy blue. 'We'll see about that,' she says, before turning on her heel and heading for the door, the others following.

'Is everything OK? Where did they go?'

I turn to see Ellie right behind me, holding my guitar.

'I don't care,' I say bitterly as I take the guitar from her. 'Those were the people who sent me the dead bird this morning.'

Ellie looks horrified and a feeling of dread drifts over from her to me. 'Oh my God! I didn't like them, but if I'd known I would have – I would have stuffed one of your aunt's vegan hotdogs right in their faces!'

I start to laugh. 'Why didn't I think of that?'

'Would I be right in thinking we have a guitarist in the house?' the lead singer of the band says over his mic. He's looking straight at me and grinning. Everyone else turns to follow his gaze.

'Yes,' Ellie cries. 'And she's brilliant.'

'Well then, why doesn't she come up and have a play with us. We love a brilliant guitarist, don't we lads?' The other members of the band laugh and nod. The boy with the fiddle grins at me again.

Ellie nudges me sharply. 'Go on,' she whispers in my ear. 'You'll get to play with Mr Seriously-Cute-With-a-Capital-C.'

I see Aunt Clara behind the counter, smiling at me and nodding.

'OK, then,' I say, feeling a weird mixture of

terror and excitement. I go over to the band. And although I don't look at him, I'm super-aware of the boy with the fiddle right next to me.

'Do you know "Hey Jude" by the Beatles?' the singer asks me.

I nod and give a little cheer inside. 'Hey Jude' is one of my dad's favourite songs. I learnt it one year so that I could play it to him for his birthday.

'Right, then.' The singer looks around at the rest of the band. 'Ready?'

'Ready,' they all call back and we start playing.

At first I feel a little awkward and tense, but it isn't long before the music has worked its usual magic on me and my fingers are flying over the guitar strings. As my confidence grows, I glance around at everyone singing and clapping along. Ellie is standing next to Aunt Clara and both of them are grinning proudly. As the song builds I can't even feel where my guitar begins and I end – it's as if we've just melted into the music. I feel so happy and alive I even pluck up the courage to glance at the boy. He looks across at exactly the same time and as our eyes meet, I feel a giddy sensation. It's coming from him too.

As the song comes to an end, Aunt Clara looks at the clock on the wall. 'It's nearly time!' she cries.

I quickly head over to Ellie and she gives me a hug. 'That was epic,' she cries. '*You* were epic!'

I hug her back and we join in the countdown to New Year's.

'Ten . . . nine . . .'

I wonder what the new year has in store for me.

'Eight . . . seven . . .'

Last year was so lousy – Dad going to Dubai, me moving to Fairhollow.

'Six . . . five . . . four . . .'

Surely next year has to be better?

'Three . . . two . . . one . . .'

As Ellie and I jump up and down, hugging each other excitedly, I feel certain that whatever the new year has in store, one thing's for certain – with my powers it's not going to be dull.

14

When my alarm clock goes off on the first day of the new term I feel equally sick and excited. I feel sick because going back to school also means having to see Izzy, Vivien and Stephen again. But I'm excited because I'll finally get to ask Holly the million and one questions I've now collected in my head about witches that felt too important to ask by text or phone. Then I remember the books on witchcraft I spotted in the shop before Christmas. Maybe I could sneak one of them out this morning? I pull on my dressing gown and creep on to the landing. There's no sound of life from downstairs and Aunt Clara's bedroom door is still shut. I tiptoe down into the shop, pull the step ladder over to the corner and grab The History of Witchcraft. Just as I'm putting the step ladder back it clatters into one of the bookcases. I freeze, waiting for Aunt Clara to call out, but the house remains silent. I tuck the book inside my dressing gown and creep back upstairs.

'What are you doing?'

Aunt Clara is standing in her bedroom doorway, in her dressing gown.

It takes every muscle in my body to stop myself from screaming.

'I was just – I thought I heard a noise in the shop.' I feel full of guilt at having to lie to her. But then a new emotion washes over me, one of suspicion and fear.

'What kind of noise?' Aunt Clara stares at me intently and the feeling of suspicion grows. It has to be coming from her.

'A sort of clattering noise. But it's OK. I checked. There's no one there.'

My guilt and her suspicion keep rolling over me in waves and I start feeling really sick. 'I'd better go and get ready for school.'

Aunt Clara doesn't say anything. She stands and watches me as I go up to my room.

I stuff the book into my school bag and throw myself down on my bed, taking long, deep breaths until the feeling of sickness fades. I wish there was some way I could control this; some way I could block out other people's feelings unless I want to know what they are. It's horrible knowing that Aunt Clara was suspicious of me. But before I can get any more stressed, my phone chimes with a new text message. It's from Holly.

Hey, do you want to meet a bit early for a chat before school? Hxx

I text back, lightning fast.

Yes! That would be great xoxo

Holly and I meet at the crossroads on the High Street. As I think about broaching the subject of witches I feel suddenly nervous. It feels like ages since the night of the school dance; it's almost like I dreamt it.

But Holly makes me feel instantly more at ease with a big hug. 'How have you been?' she asks.

'OK. I think. It's a lot to get my head around. I've really missed being able to talk to you face-to-face.'

Holly sighs. 'Me too! I had a terrible time in Austria. I couldn't tell you around Ellie, but on the last day I had this major row with my dad about which is best, the Harry Potter books or the movies.' She looks suddenly indignant, 'He actually thinks the movies are better! But movies are never better than the books they're based on. Ever! Anyway, I got really cross with him and I ended up blowing up the ski lift.'

I stare at her. 'What?'

Holly shrugs. 'Well, I didn't exactly blow it up, but it blew a fuse, right when I got really mad at him, so I know it was my fault.' Holly looks around sadly. 'We were stuck up there for hours. It was a nightmare. Normally when I have a row with one of my parents my favourite bit is storming off after. But I had to sit up there with him in silence until they got it running again, which took forever. I just wish . . .' She breaks off and looks away.

'What?'

'I wish there was some way I could control this thing, you know? I wish Grandma was still around to explain it.'

'Yes! Me too.' I reach in my bag for the book. 'I found this in my aunt's shop. It's not exactly your grandma, but I thought it might help us.'

'*The History of Witchcraft*,' Holly reads from the cover. 'Well, it's got to be worth a go.'

But it just takes a quick flick through the index to see that the book won't be any help. It doesn't say anything about the kind of powers we have and it doesn't mention Fairhollow at all.

I sigh. It's so frustrating.

'Don't worry,' Holly says, linking arms with me as we turn into the school driveway. 'There has to be something somewhere.'

As soon as we get to our form room and I see Izzy, I feel a wave of hatred so strong I find it hard to breathe. I sit down at my desk at the front of the class with Holly and feel the hatred stabbing into my back like daggers. I try to calm myself by thinking happy thoughts, but the mix of emotions only make me feel sick.

The first lesson after registration is Maths. This is bad for three reasons. First, I'm in a different set to Holly. Second, I'm in the same set as Izzy and Vivien. And third, I have to sit right in front of them. With Izzy so close behind me it feels as if every cell in my body is being eaten up by loathing. As our teacher, Miss Banks, starts writing equations on the whiteboard I can't concentrate at all. I find algebra bad at the best of times, but now all the Xs and the Ys are forming a red blur of anger and hate.

I look down at my book and force myself to copy the equations. For a moment this seems to work. Focusing on the letters and numbers makes the hatred fade a little.

'Does anyone have anything to say before we begin the exercise?' Miss Banks asks, with her back towards us, still writing on the whiteboard.

'Yes, Miss,' I hear a voice say. I hear *my* voice say! 'Why are you so crap at teaching?'

I sit open-mouthed in shock as Miss Banks spins around, and stares at me. 'What did you just say, Nessa?'

'I didn't –' I stammer. 'It wasn't me.'

I hear Vivien snigger behind me.

'It wasn't you?' Miss Banks starts walking towards me, her face flushed with anger. 'Of course it was you. I recognised your accent.'

'But I – it must have been someone doing an impression of me.'

'Oh, really?' Miss Banks is standing right in front of me now and I can feel the anger coming off her like a furnace. Combined with the hatred coming from behind me it makes my stomach churn like crazy. 'So, are you saying there's a ventriloquist in the class, Miss Reid?'

'No – I – yes.' My face flushes as the rest of the class start sniggering.

'Silence!' Miss Banks snaps. Then she glares back at me. 'I have no time for comedians in my classroom, Miss Reid. Do you understand?'

I nod. She marches back to her desk and produces a yellow card. 'Maybe this will help focus your mind and make you appreciate my teaching skills,' she says, handing it to me.

I look at the card blankly, not sure what I'm supposed to do with it.

'A yellow card is a warning,' Miss Banks explains. 'You need to give it to your form tutor at registration. Two yellow cards equal a suspension.'

As I look down at the card I start bubbling with anger, this time my own, coming from deep inside of me. It must have been Izzy or Vivien who did that impression of me. But how?

'Ah, poor Nessa,' I hear Ellie whisper behind me as Miss Banks walks back to her desk. 'It's so unfair.'

Ellie! I spin round to see Vivien grinning at me, her eyes glinting.

'What's the matter?' she asks coldly.

I turn back and look down at my book, my head a jumble of confusion.

At lunch break, I meet up with Holly and lead her straight to the library.

'We have to try and see if we can find anything online,' I say. 'I need to know more about all of this right now!'

'What's happened?' Holly asks, looking really concerned.

'Are some witches able to mimic other people's voices?' I whisper as we enter the library.

Holly nods slowly. 'Yes, I think I remember my grandma mentioning that. Why?'

'I think that might be Vivien's special power. She used it in maths and got me into loads of trouble.'

I open my bag and take out a book on music that I borrowed before the Christmas break. 'Can I return this, please?' I say to the librarian, handing it to her. 'Go and get a computer,' I say to Holly. 'We need to start searching.'

'Excuse me.'

I look back at the librarian. 'Yes?'

'Is this some kind of joke?' She holds the book out to me. The front cover is covered in red scrawl. The librarian opens the book and starts flicking through. There are slashes of red ink throughout. 'You can't deface school property like this,' she says, looking horrified.

'I – I didn't,' I stammer. 'I mean, it was fine when I put it in my bag this morning.'

'Whose form are you in?' The librarian looks at me sternly.

'Mr Matthews. But I didn't do this, honestly.' I look at Holly, hoping she can say or do something to help.

'She didn't,' Holly says. 'She loves music – and books – her aunt runs a bookshop. So she'd never deface a book – it would be against her religion, if loving music and books was a religion.' Holly gives me a helpless smile.

'The damage happened in your care,' the librarian says, staring at me angrily. 'I can't believe you had the nerve to return it looking like this.'

'She's under a lot of pressure at the moment,' Holly says desperately.

'She certainly will be,' the librarian says, producing a yellow card from her desk, 'when her form tutor finds out about this.'

'This is totally unfair,' Holly cries. 'It's an injustice, a breach of her rights as a card-carrying library member. My parents are lawyers, they know about these things.'

'Enough,' the librarian says, holding up her hand like she's stopping traffic. 'Miss Reid, take this card to your form tutor please.'

I take the card from her.

'But –' Holly begins.

I grab hold of her arm. 'It's OK. Come on.'

When we get to the form room and I give my yellow cards to Mr Matthews he looks really shocked and, unlike Miss Banks and the librarian, I feel nothing but concern from him.

'Well, well, this is most unexpected,' he says, scratching his head. 'Is everything OK, Nessa?'

'No, it's –' Holly begins but I nudge her to shut up.

'It's fine,' I mutter.

'Are you sure?' Mr Matthews stares at me like he wants me to tell him more. But how can I? He'd probably give me an entire pack of yellow cards for being a crazy person.

'Yes,' I say.

Mr Matthews looks genuinely upset. 'Well, in that case, I'm afraid I have no choice but to suspend you for the rest of the day. It's the school rules – two yellow cards equal a temporary suspension.'

'The school rules suck,' Holly mutters.

'Then I'll let your aunt know,' Mr Matthews continues. 'She'll need to come and get you.'

My heart sinks.

'Are you absolutely sure there's nothing else you want to tell me?' He looks at me hopefully.

I shake my head. 'No, sir.'

Mr Matthews sighs. 'OK then, go and wait in reception and I'll call your aunt.'

Holly gives my hand a comforting squeeze as we leave the room. 'This is so unfair!'

I nod. 'Yep.'

When we get to the stairwell Izzy, Vivien and Stephen are walking up towards us. As soon as they see us they start to smirk.

'I told you we'd make your life hell,' Izzy sneers as she barges past me.

My arm feels as cold as ice where she touches it.

If a TV company ever decides to make a show called World's Most Awkward Car Journeys they need to give me and Aunt Clara a call. Our drive back from school is excruciating. The worst thing is, she doesn't say a word about what I've done, or what I'm supposed to have done, or what the Head said to her when she was called into his office. But all the way back I can sense her disappointment hanging between us like a thick heavy cloud.

'I need to go into Newbridge to pick up some stock,' she says flatly, as we pull up outside Paper Soul. 'I'll be back about six and we'll talk then.'

'OK,' I say, wishing I could say something to make her feel better but knowing that I can't. I get out of the car. As soon as I shut the door behind me I relax a bit. It's like I've shut the heavy sense of disappointment into the car with her. I unlock the door to Paper Soul and step into the gloom. As soon as I see Aunt Clara drive off, I put *The History of Witchcraft* back on its shelf. Then I trudge into the café area and sit down at one of the tables. What happened today has changed everything. I have to find out more about exactly what Izzy, Vivien and Stephen's powers are, and I have to find out more about my powers as a witch too, so I know how to deal with them. I look around the shop. It's weirdly peaceful in the gloom. I think back to the New Year's Eve party, playing guitar with the band right where I'm now sitting, feeling so happy and carefree. I get the sudden urge to play my guitar again, just to have a break from the stress. I'm about to go upstairs and get it when I hear a tap on the door. I decide to ignore it as we're closed, but whoever it is keeps on knocking. Then my phone chimes with a text.

It's me! Let me in! Hxx

I rush over to the door. Holly's standing outside with the hood of her coat pulled right down low over her face.

'What are you doing here?' I ask as I open the door. Holly slips past me into the shop.

'I had to make sure you were OK.'

'But won't you get into trouble for skipping school?'

'I told them I was sick.' Holly looks at me. 'And I wasn't lying. I am sick. Sick of Izzy and the others. We have to start fighting back.' Her eyes glint in the darkness and I feel her sense of determination. 'It's never been so important that we learn how to use our powers properly.'

'I know, but how?'

I lead Holly over to the café area and we sit down.

'We need to practise, like we're athletes training

for the Olympics or something. Look what I can already do.' Holly glances at a portable heater over in the corner. Then she starts staring at it really intently. One by one, the bars on the heater start glowing orange, then bright red. The room fills with heat.

'Wow, that's awesome,' I say, with a laugh.

Holly doesn't say anything and keeps on staring at the heater. A bead of sweat forms on her forehead and trickles down the side of her face. It's starting to get really hot now.

I take my school blazer off. 'OK, maybe a little bit too awesome.'

Holly lets out a gasp and shuts her eyes. The bars on the heater start to dim. 'It's so frustrating!' she says. 'There must be loads more I can do with my power, but I just don't know.'

'Well, at least you didn't make anything blow up this time,' I say, trying to console her. 'That's something.'

'Yeah, great.' Holly mutters. 'Do you want to have a go at reading my feelings again?'

I frown. 'To be honest. I think I'd rather learn

how to stop feeling them. Whenever I pick up any strong feeling it makes me feel really sick, especially when I'm near Izzy. I need to learn how to block her hatred out.'

Holly nods thoughtfully. 'OK, well, why don't I make myself feel something and you practise blocking it?'

She moves round the table so she's sitting directly opposite me. 'Right, let me know when you start picking something up.'

I nod and close my eyes and suddenly I'm hit by a wave of anger. 'Wow, what are you thinking about?'

'Izzy,' Holly says bitterly.

'OK, I'm definitely feeling it.'

'Good. Now you have to focus on blocking it out. Why don't you picture a big wall around you or something?'

I picture a wall around me but if anything it only makes things worse, like I'm trapped behind it with Holly's anger. Then I remember the Maths lesson and how I'd started to make Izzy's hatred fade when

171

I concentrated on the algebra. As there's no way I want to be doing algebra every time this happens, I decide to focus on something else. Something nicer, something more positive. Something that makes me feel safe and strong. Instantly, a picture of the old oak tree forms in my mind. I think of its strong roots, of nestling between them and absorbing the strength of the tree. Straightaway, I feel a bit better. It's as if Holly's anger is being pushed back out of me by the tree's strength. I keep on focusing until it feels as if I *am* the tree, my roots digging right down into the ground. Holly's anger is just like tiny pinpricks at the ends of my fingers now. I feel amazing.

'What's happening?' Holly asks.

I open my eyes and look at her.

'I was still thinking about Izzy but you were really grinning,' she says.

'I think I've found a way to block it,' I say. 'Test me again, with another feeling.'

This time, I feel a wave of sadness coming from Holly. It sweeps into me, making my heart ache. I try keeping my eyes open this time and picture the tree right in front of me. Then I imagine myself leaning against the trunk, soaking up its strength, and bit by bit the sadness fades. When it's totally gone I look at Holly. 'That was sadness, right?'

Holly nods. 'Yes, I was thinking of the day my grandma died.'

I place my hand over hers on the table and give it a squeeze. 'I managed to block it,' I say softly and I feel a weight lifting from my shoulders. If I can block Izzy's poisonous feelings I'll be able to focus on fighting back.

'That's awesome,' Holly says, a smile lighting up her face. 'Hey – there's one more thing that I remember my grandma saying about empaths. She told me that sometimes they can control other people's minds.'

I gape at her. 'What do you mean?'

'Apparently picking up on a person's feelings is just one part of being an empath. They can get inside people's minds too.'

'What? But why didn't you tell me this before?'

Holly shrugs. 'I thought it might have been a bit too much to deal with.'

'Fair enough. But how am I supposed to control someone else's mind? That sounds really hard.'

Holly frowns. 'I guess you have to really want them to do something and focus all of your attention on it.'

I get a sudden flashback to the night of the school dance and a shiver runs up my spine. I stare at Holly. 'Do you think that's what happened at the dance? When Izzy fell over? I remember really wanting her to get away from me.'

'Yes!' Holly's eyes light up 'Oh my God! You must have controlled her mind without realising it. This is epic!' She jumps to her feet and comes to stand in front of me. 'Come on.'

'What?'

'Try doing it to me, now.'

'No! I don't want to make you fall over.'

Holly sighs. 'OK then. Try and make me jump

up and down on the spot.'

I laugh. 'All right.' I close my eyes and focus really hard on Holly jumping up and down. 'Anything?' I say, after a few seconds, opening my eyes.

Holly shakes her head. 'Imagine you *have* to make me do it.'

I close my eyes and picture Holly jumping up and down in order to save a kitten stuck in a tree. 'Anything?'

She shakes her head.

'Not even the slightest feeling that you want to jump up and down?'

'No, sorry.'

I'm just about to try again when I hear a key in the shop's front door. We look at each other in horror.

'Aunt Clara!' I gasp.

'Is there a back door?' Holly whispers.

'Yes. Quick.'

We race through the kitchen to the storeroom at the very back of the shop.

'I'll see you in school tomorrow,' Holly whispers and she hugs me tight. 'Silver Witches forever,' she whispers in my ear.

And once again I get a weird shiver going up my spine. But this time it isn't fear. Now I've realised that I can control some of my power it doesn't feel so scary at all. In fact, it feels kind of exciting.

16

I used to think I'd had a bad week if I got set double Physics homework, but now I realise that I didn't know the true meaning of a bad week at all. It's now Friday and I'm sitting in my favourite chair outside the Head's office. The fact that I have a favourite chair outside the Head's office is one sign of just how bad this week has been. Another is the fact that Aunt Clara is sitting beside me, waiting to see the Head too. Since I returned to school on Tuesday, Izzy, Vivien and Stephen have been working on their own extra-curricular project called 'Make Nessa's Life Hell'. In English, Vivien mimicked me yelling that 'Shakespeare sucks'.

In French, Izzy somehow managed to scrawl pictures of berets and strings of onions all over my homework – after I'd handed it in. And in Biology, a vital piece of coursework on the reproductive systems of plants vanished from my folder.

The headmaster's secretary comes out of her office and smiles at Aunt Clara. She never smiles at me, even though I see her every day.

'OK, Miss Hamilton, Mr Bailey is ready to see you.'

Nervousness shimmers from Aunt Clara as she stands up, instantly making me feel super guilty. I quickly picture the oak tree before the clashing emotions get too much. The one good thing about this week is that I've got loads better at blocking other people's feelings. Izzy and the others have given me plenty of practice.

I trudge after Aunt Clara into Mr Bailey's office. He's standing behind his desk with a weary expression on his face.

'Hello, Miss Hamilton,' he says to Aunt Clara,

before looking at me. 'Nessa.'

'Hello, sir.'

He gestures to the chairs on the other side of his desk and we all sit down.

'So, as I'm sure you're aware from the letter I sent you yesterday, we've been having some real problems with Nessa this week,' Mr Bailey says to Aunt Clara.

Everything about Mr Bailey is super neat, from his immaculately-clipped hair to his perfectly-arranged desk.

'Yes, I'm so sorry to hear that,' Aunt Clara says. Sorrow and stress seep from her into me like a cold mist.

I feel another pang of guilt and quickly focus on my tree and its strong roots.

'We're very sorry too,' Mr Bailey says. 'She'd got off to such a promising start here.'

One of my biggest pet hates is when adults talk about you as if you aren't even in the room. I try really hard to keep myself from frowning.

'Her form tutor, Mr Matthews, is particularly upset.' Mr Bailey moves a folder on his desk one millimetre to the left. 'He says she'd settled in really well before the Christmas break.'

'Maybe Fairhollow High just isn't a good fit for her,' Aunt Clara says. 'Maybe we should think about moving her to Newbridge?'

'What?!' I'm so horrified I can't help saying it out loud. They both turn to look at me. Mr Bailey raises his eyebrows in surprise, like he'd forgotten I was even here.

'Things clearly aren't going right for you here.' Aunt Clara says. 'Maybe a fresh new start somewhere else is what you need.'

'But I don't want a fresh new start. I've only just arrived in Fairhollow!' Panic starts bubbling up inside of me as I think about leaving Holly. 'I want to stay here.'

'But all of your actions would indicate that you don't want to stay here,' Mr Bailey says. 'You've been warned repeatedly about your behaviour this week but you keep being disruptive.'

'I don't, I . . .' I break off, feeling close to tears with frustration.

Aunt Clara looks at me intently and I feel a wave of concern. 'Is there something you aren't telling us, Nessa?'

I shake my head and look down at my lap.

'Why don't we all have a think about it over the weekend,' Mr Bailey says, his voice softer, 'and we can decide what to do on Monday?'

Aunt Clara nods. 'Thank you. I'll give Newbridge High a ring this afternoon. See if they have any places.'

It takes all my concentration not to yell with frustration. As Aunt Clara and Mr Bailey stand up and shake hands I march out of the office. This is all so unfair.

'Nessa!' Aunt Clara calls after me.

'What?' I don't even turn round, I just keep on striding through reception and out of the main exit. All of the other students are long gone and the driveway is deserted. The sky is dark grey, perfectly matching my mood.

'I don't understand what's going on with you,' Aunt Clara says as she catches up with me.

'I don't want to go to Newbridge.' I stare at the ground sullenly.

Aunt Clara takes her keys from her pocket and bleeps her car unlocked. 'Come on, let's go home and talk about this over a nice cup of tea.'

'I don't want a nice cup of tea!' I'm aware that I'm talking like a spoilt kid but I can't help it. The thought of leaving Holly – of leaving Holly on her own with Izzy and the others – is horrible.

'Nessa, please!' Aunt Clara opens the passenger door for me to get in.

I shake my head. 'I don't want to come with you. I want to be on my own.'

'But . . .'

'Just leave me alone.' I turn and start running down the darkening driveway, tears burning my eyes.

I keep on running until I get to the oak tree. I fling myself on to the icy ground and lean against the trunk. Once again, it's as if the tree's hugging me. The feeling's even stronger now, maybe because I've been picturing the tree so often when I'm blocking out other people's emotions. I close my eyes and take a few deep breaths until my heart rate goes back to normal. What am I going to do? I can't let Aunt Clara and Mr Bailey move me to another school. I can't leave Holly. But how can I stop Izzy and the others from getting me into trouble? It's not enough to protect myself from their hatred. I have to fight back, the way Holly talked about. If only becoming a witch came with some kind of instruction manual. If only Holly's grandma had given her more information. If only . . .

I hear the crunch of footsteps coming up the path and I freeze. What if it's Izzy and the others? What if they saw me and followed me here? I can't bear the thought of them discovering my safe place. When I see Aunt Clara appear I'm actually relieved.

'How – how did you know I was here?' I stammer.

'I followed you.' As Aunt Clara walks over to me I'm filled by a wave of love. It warms me right through like one of her steaming mugs of ginger tea. 'Come on,' she says gently, holding out her hand. 'Let's go and get some sticky toffee pudding.'

'But – but Paper Soul doesn't do sticky toffee pudding.' I take hold of her hand and she helps me up.

'We aren't going to Paper Soul,' she says with a smile. 'Some days you just need sugar, right?'

I nod and smile. 'Right.'

*

Aunt Clara takes me to The Cup and Saucer. It's so warm the windows have steamed up and it's full of chatter and laughter. It reminds me of the café I used to go to every Saturday morning with Dad after we did the food shop. My eyes instantly fill with tears.

I'm still feeling emotional after we've sat down and ordered our puddings.

'Are you OK?' Aunt Clara says, staring at me across the table. Feeling her concern only makes me want to cry even more. All week, I've tried so hard to stay strong but the warmth of the café and Aunt Clara's genuine concern are melting away my defences.

'Yes, I – it's just –' The tears that have been building in my eyes spill on to my face. As I try wiping them away someone places a bowl on the table in front of me. Someone wearing a black leather friendship bracelet. I look up and see the boy from the band. He's wearing a waiter's uniform

185

and a pen is poking out of his curly black hair, tucked behind his ear.

'Hello again,' he says with a grin. 'Two sticky toffee puddings.' He places another bowl in front of Aunt Clara then he looks back at me, concerned. 'Oh – are you OK?'

My face flushes so hot I'm amazed the tears don't turn to steam.

'Here.' He hands me a napkin. 'The food here's not that bad, honest,' he says with a grin and his green eyes sparkle. 'Especially the sticky toffee pudding. The sticky toffee pudding's amazing.'

I start half-laughing, half-crying, which is possibly the most unattractive thing a person can do, but thankfully he doesn't look repulsed. He just hands me another napkin. 'I tell you what, have it on the house,' he nods at the pudding, 'or on me, anyway.'

'Really?' I smile up at him through my tears.

'Yes.' Now his face is flushing and he quickly looks away. 'I'd better get back. I'll make sure they only charge you for the drinks.'

Aunt Clara and I watch in silence as he heads back to the counter.

'Well, well, maybe things aren't so bad after all,' Aunt Clara says with a chuckle. 'Looks like you've got yourself an admirer.'

I look at her and smile. But it's impossible for me to feel really happy. It's as if Izzy and the others have placed a curse on me. No matter how cute the boy from the band is and how much sticky toffee pudding he buys me, all I can think is, what about Holly?

'They might make you move schools?' Holly stops walking and stares at me, her eyes saucer-wide with shock.

It's Saturday morning and we're on our way to the library. Officially to do our homework on our own, unofficially to try and find out more about the witches of Fairhollow together.

I'd decided to save telling Holly the terrible news until we were face to face, but now, seeing her horrified expression, I'm kind of wishing I'd texted instead.

'My aunt thinks I need *another* fresh start.'

Holly shakes her head in disbelief. 'But where?'

'Newbridge.'

Holly shudders. 'You can't. You can't leave. You're – you're my best friend.' She looks down and scuffs her foot against the pavement. 'I know we've only known each other a few weeks – and it's OK, I know Ellie's your best friend – but you're the first person I've met that I've ever wanted to be best friends with. Other girls can be so awful. But you're not. You're awesome. And you're a . . .' – she looks at me – '. . . you know. Like me.'

I nod. 'It's like having a sister isn't it? It's like we've got this bond.'

'Yes.' She takes hold of my hands and stares at me defiantly. 'You can't move schools. We have to do something.'

I nod. 'Exactly. That's why I suggested going to the library again. We need to find out more, so that we can fight back.'

Holly lets go of my hands and starts marching along the street. 'Absolutely. Come on!'

*

The trouble with living in a small town like Fairhollow is that the library is *the* place to be on a Saturday morning. When we get there it's packed with mums and little kids and every computer is taken. We put our names down on the list for one, then go searching for books. We find a couple on witchcraft and take them over to a quiet corner in the non-fiction section.

'Mine's rubbish,' Holly whispers. 'It's all about America.'

I nod. 'Mine's no good either. It's like reading a history book.'

Finally, we get on a computer. This time, I do a search for 'Fairhollow Blood Witches and Silver Witches'. One result comes up; a link to one of those prehistoric websites that looks as if it's been designed by someone's granddad, with garish colours and handwriting-style fonts. The website's called FAIRHOLLOW FORUM and the link sends us to a discussion page titled: *Has anyone heard of the Blood Witches and Silver Witches that were supposed to have lived in Fairhollow?* There are just two comments posted below. The first one, from someone called **BakerPete**, just says '*nope*'.

'Helpful,' Holly mutters.

But the second comment, from someone called **Mary223**, is quite a bit longer. Holly and I move closer to the screen to read it.

When I was little, my mum used to tell me stories about the witches who lived in Fairhollow hundreds of years ago. There were two groups, the Blood Witches and the Silver Witches. The Blood Witches were the baddies and the Silver Witches were the goodies. But it's just town folkore. I don't think they actually existed . . .

'Ha, that's what she thinks.' Holly sighs and looks at me. 'So what do we do now?'

'We could post a comment, asking for more information.' I try to type a reply but a message comes up saying that the moderator has closed the thread. Then I notice the time in the corner of the screen. 'Oh no! I have to go and help out in the shop.' I push my chair back and pick up my bag.

'I can't get into trouble with Aunt Clara this weekend or she'll never let me stay at Fairhollow High.'

Holly looks at me helplessly. 'What are we going to do?'

'We have to look somewhere else. Somewhere older. Books *have* to be the answer. We just haven't found the right one yet.'

As we head to the door I only wish I feel as hopeful as I sound.

19

For the rest of the weekend I'm on Mission: Keep Aunt Clara Happy. I volunteer for dishes duty in the café on Saturday afternoon. Saturday evening I clean the bathroom and my bedroom – without being asked – and on Sunday I spend hours over my History homework, an essay on Anne Boleyn. By Monday morning, as I make my way up the High Street to meet Holly, I'm exhausted, but at least Aunt Clara hasn't mentioned me moving schools again.

In the early morning gloom I can just make out Holly leaning against a lamppost by the crossroads. 'Well?' she says, looking at me hopefully.

'OK – I think. She hasn't said anything more about me going to Newbridge.'

'Yay!' Holly claps her hands excitedly and the orange glow from the streetlight flickers. 'Whoops!'

We both look at each other and laugh.

'So now I just have to make sure Izzy and the others don't cause me any more problems.' I sigh.

Holly frowns. 'Yeah, well, if they do they'll have me to deal with.' She looks up at the streetlight again and crinkles her nose. The light flashes on and off. 'I've been practising,' Holly says with a grin as we start walking along the road. 'You should have seen what happened yesterday when I went out for dinner with my parents. We went to this fancy-schmancy restaurant in Newbridge and it had this electric water feature in the corner, you know, like a little waterfall.'

'Oh no,' I say with a grin. 'Don't tell me, you drowned half the diners?'

'No!' Holly giggles. 'Well, only one of them. I was trying to make the waterfall go a bit faster but it

194

ended up shooting into the air like a fireman's hose and it went all over this man's head. He went crazy, shouting at all the waiters. It turns out my parents knew him – he was the judge on a case they worked on. He didn't rule in their favour so Dad was really happy he got drenched.'

We're still laughing when we get into school.

'What's so funny?'

I stop dead at the sound of Stephen's voice behind us.

'None of your business,' I say, turning to face him. I feel an icy blast of contempt coming off him, but I quickly think of the oak tree and it fades.

Stephen takes a step closer and scowls at me. It's weird. On the surface he looks like the perfect Hollywood heartthrob with his bright blue eyes, floppy blond hair and chiselled cheekbones, but the hatred oozing out of him makes him look really ugly – to me anyway.

'Yeah, well, you won't be laughing when you

have to go to Newbridge, will you?' Stephen turns and scowls at Holly. 'Poor little Holly. It's taken you all this time to find a friend and now you're going to be all alone again.'

I feel a bolt of anger and go to grab his arm, but Holly pulls me away.

'It's not worth it,' she whispers and I somehow manage to calm myself down. Stephen laughs right in my face before running up the stairs two at a time. I stare after him, in shock. The only people who know about Newbridge are me, Holly, Aunt Clara and Mr Bailey. I look at Holly. She's staring after Stephen looking really mad. 'How does he know?' I whisper.

She shrugs. 'Maybe it's something to with his power?'

'What, to know everything?'

'It could be. But he *doesn't* know everything,' Holly says angrily. 'And it's about time someone made him realise that.' She starts marching up the stairs. I follow close behind, wondering what she means.

In registration, even the discovery that Izzy and Vivien are both off today doing work experience doesn't do anything to calm my unease. How has Stephen found out that I might be moving schools?

The first lesson after registration is Chemistry. 'OK, everyone,' Miss Phillips says loudly as we set up our test tubes, 'start gently heating the contents of your tubes over your Bunsen burners.'

I look at Holly, wondering why her test tube isn't next to mine over the flame. She's staring at Stephen at the front of the class. Like, *really* staring and crinkling her nose, the same way as she did at the streetlight earlier. The Bunsen burner in front of Stephen makes a weird hissing sound and its flame leaps up.

'Whoa!' Stephen yells, jumping backwards. The classroom's filled with the tinkle of broken glass as the test tube he was holding crashes to the floor.

'Ew, what's that smell?' one of the girls in front of us asks, holding her nose.

'My eyebrows!' Stephen yells, clapping a hand to his forehead.

I look back at Holly. She's grinning so hard her dimples are on full display.

'What happened?' Miss Phillips says, rushing over to Stephen.

As Stephen turns to face her, it takes every muscle I've got not to start laughing. His eyebrows have been totally singed off, making his forehead look huge, like Frankenstein's Monster.

'I don't know, Miss,' Stephen says, his voice all trembling and pitiful. 'The Bunsen burner went crazy.' He pats at his forehead, looking really upset. 'What's happened to my eyebrows?'

'Oh dear, I'm afraid they've been burnt off,' Miss Phillips says, looking really concerned. 'You're lucky your face wasn't burnt too. We should get you to the nurse straightaway.'

Stephen looks grief-stricken.

'Don't worry, Stephen,' the girl next to him says in a sappy voice. 'You still look awesome.'

'Yes,' a handful of other girls begin cooing like pigeons.

'But my eyebrows,' he says mournfully.

Holly winks at me. 'High five,' she whispers, offering me her hand under the table.

'High five,' I whisper back, my entire body feeling like one giant grin.

20

The rest of the day goes really well. With Izzy and Vivien both away and Stephen in mourning for his cremated eyebrows I'm able to focus on my work and try to make up for everything that went wrong last week. I get a full house of ticks and nice comments on my report card and when I go to show Mr Matthews at the end of the day he smiles at me and says, 'Well done, Nessa, I'm very proud of you.' It makes me happy and sad. Happy because I feel like I've made my case for staying at Fairhollow High a lot stronger, and sad because it's the kind of thing Dad would say and it makes me miss him.

I'm still missing Dad as I make my way back home along the High Street. I glance across the road to The Cup and Saucer. The boy from the band is clearing one of the tables outside. My heart starts fluttering like it's grown a pair of fairy wings. *Look over at me*, I think as I watch him, and he puts down his cloth and looks right at me. My cheeks flush and I quickly look away. It's official – I'm the world's most awkward girl when it comes to boys. Then I think about how he looked over the minute I wanted him to and it makes the hairs on the back of my neck stand on end. It has to be a coincidence. I spent all weekend trying to make Aunt Clara cough or yawn or stretch and it didn't work at all.

'No sticky toffee pudding today then?' the boy calls to me across the road.

I look back at him. He's standing there, grinning. My heart now seems to have taken up tap-dancing.

'Er – no – not today,' I call back, my voice all stiff with embarrassment.

'Shame,' he says, just as a car drives past.

'Sorry!' I call.

'Sorry?' He looks really confused.

'Yes.' My face is burning now.

'Your name is sorry?'

'What? Oh – no. I thought you said "shame".'

He looks at me blankly. I pray for a bus to drive up so that I can hide behind.

'I said, what's your name?' he calls.

'Nessa. Bye,' I say quickly, hurrying off before my face actually bursts into flames.

'Hi, Nessa-Bye. I'm Niall. See you again soon,' he calls after me.

I don't turn back because I don't want him to see how much I'm smiling.

I'm still smiling when I get back to Paper Soul.

Monday is Aunt Clara's day off and so the shop is shut and steeped in darkness. I let myself in and go straight upstairs, humming the latest song I've been working on. I'm about to get juice from the fridge when I notice an envelope on the kitchen table. It's addressed to 'the Guardian of Nessa

Reid'. My heart sinks. I pick up the envelope and turn it over. It's unsealed.

In my list of things you should never, ever do, reading someone else's mail is up there alongside drowning puppies. But this is an emergency. This letter could contain my future happiness, or rather, unhappiness – and besides, it does have my name on the envelope. Surely that makes it a bit better? Going over to the kitchen door so that I can hear any sound of Aunt Clara returning, I quickly slide the letter out and unfold it. It's from Mr Bailey. The heading reads:

Re: Nessa Reid's transfer from Fairhollow High to Newbridge High

This time, my heart doesn't just sink, it feels as if it's plummeted to the very centre of the earth. The letter goes on to say that there are places available at Newbridge High and that Mr Bailey thinks I ought to move there as soon as possible.

'Under the circumstances a speedy transfer will be in Nessa's best interests,' he finishes. At the bottom of the letter there's a slip for Aunt Clara to sign, giving her permission for me to move schools. I swallow hard. My mouth's gone really dry. In my 'best interests'? Making me move away from Holly would be in my very *worst* interests. I put the letter back in the envelope and place it exactly where it was on the table. The last thing I need is Aunt Clara discovering that I've been reading her mail. Panic flutters inside me like a trapped bird. What am I going to do?

Instantly, I think of Dad. I hadn't told him what happened last week because I didn't want to worry him but now I've got no choice. Maybe he can persuade Aunt Clara to change her mind. I go up to my room, as far away from the letter as possible, and try calling him. But my call goes straight to voicemail. I feel a pang of sorrow and frustration. What with his long shifts and the time difference it's so hard getting hold of him. But I haven't got time to feel sorry for myself. I need to do something now, so I call Holly instead.

Fifteen minutes later, Holly and I are sliding into a booth in The Cup and Saucer. There's no sign of Niall – but that's probably a very good thing as I need all of my powers of concentration.

'So, what exactly did the letter say?' Holly asks, looking deadly serious.

I quote it word for word, before ordering a milkshake from the waitress.

'And has your aunt signed it?' Holly asks when she's gone away again.

I shake my head. 'No. Not yet.'

Holly looks hopeful. 'Maybe she won't. Maybe she's changed her mind.'

'Maybe. But what about Mr Bailey? What if he hasn't? What if he's decided he wants me to go? It certainly seemed like that from his letter.'

Holly shakes her head. 'Maybe he felt like that when he wrote it, but he'll soon change his mind when he hears how you got on today. You did great in all your lessons.'

'Yes, but that's only because Izzy and Vivien were off.' I sigh. 'As soon as they get back they'll be making my life hell again and I can't do anything to stop them. Oh no!' I slide down in my chair as I spot Aunt Clara walking in.

'What is it?' Holly turns round to look at the door.

'No! Don't turn round. Don't let her see you.'

But it's too late. Aunt Clara's staring over at our booth and she isn't smiling. She's the opposite of smiling. I hold my breath, hoping that by some miracle she hasn't realised it's me. I grab a menu to hide behind.

'Nessa?' Aunt Clara calls.

'Don't worry, it'll be OK,' Holly whispers.

'Why couldn't my power be invisibility?' I wail, keeping my nose buried in the menu.

'Nessa!' Aunt Clara's voice is icy sharp as she reaches the table. 'What are you doing?'

'We're just having milkshakes,' Holly says cheerily, 'and talking about homework.'

'Get up,' Aunt Clara says to me. 'Now!' She grabs hold of my arm really tightly and pulls me up. A picture flashes into my head. A grave. *Mum's* grave. And Aunt Clara standing by it with tears pouring down her face.

'But I . . .'

Aunt Clara pulls me harder.

Holly stares up at us, open-mouthed.

'I'm sorry,' I say to her, my heart pounding. 'I have to go.'

'What are you doing?' I cry as Aunt Clara frog-marches me up the High Street. 'What were *you* doing? she hisses. 'I told you not to spend time with her!'

'I don't get it!' I say. 'Why do you hate her so much?'

'I told you – she's bad news. No wonder you've been getting into so much trouble at school.'

I try to unlink my arm from Aunt Clara's but she's gripping it too tightly. I feel anger and hurt pouring into me from her and I'm so confused I forget to block it. Why did I see a picture of Mum's grave? I must have picked it up from Aunt Clara, but why would she be thinking of Mum when she saw me with Holly? It doesn't make any sense. I start feeling really sick, which isn't helped any when I see Izzy and Vivien smirking at me from the bench outside the hairdressers.

'Are you OK?' Aunt Clara stops walking and looks at me. She doesn't let go of my arm, though.

'No. I feel sick. Can we please just go home?' As we walk past Izzy and Vivien I don't look anywhere near them, but I feel their hatred cutting into me like knives.

By the time we get back to Paper Soul I feel really drained. We go upstairs in silence and sit down at the kitchen table. I focus on my breathing and picturing the oak tree until I feel slightly better.

Aunt Clara places a mug of camomile tea in front of me. 'Drink this,' she says.

I take a sip and relax slightly as the tea makes a warm trail down my throat.

'You have to trust me, Nessa,' Aunt Clara says,

sitting down opposite me. 'I only want what's best for you.'

I look down at my lap. 'But I like Holly.'

'You have to stay away from her.' Aunt Clara's voice goes shrill with tension. I don't understand why she's being so cruel. Holly's my only friend – why won't she let me keep her?

'But I don't want to stay away from her, and I don't want to move schools. It's been hard enough moving up here. I don't want any more upheaval.' I look at her imploringly. 'Please.'

Aunt Clara looks away. A cloud of confusion drifts towards me across the table and I feel a glimmer of hope. She's not angry, she's upset. Maybe she still isn't sure what to do. Maybe I can convince her to change her mind. Maybe if I pretend I'm willing to stop seeing Holly, she'll let me stay.

'If I promise I won't have anything to do with Holly, please can I stay at Fairhollow?'

Aunt Clara sighs. 'Maybe. Let me think about it.'

'OK.'

'I need to know that I can trust you not to have anything to do with her.'

'You can.' It hurts me to say it, but I know I have to.

She looks at me and sighs. 'I'll think about it.'

I leap up from my chair and rush round the table to hug her. 'Thank you.'

'I only said I'll think about it.' Aunt Clara sits there stiffly, but I can feel a glow of love coming from her. 'If I hear from the school that there's been any more trouble . . .'

'You won't,' I say, mentally crossing all of my fingers and trying to ignore my feelings of guilt.

The next morning, I wake up extra early to help Aunt Clara do some baking. She's hosting a book launch at Paper Soul tonight and she needs a ton of snacks for the buffet. As I weigh out some ground almonds, I glance over at her. She's got a bowl nestled in the crook of her arm and she's mixing up some cake batter. She looks as if she's miles away and there's a gentle smile on her face. The only time I ever see Aunt Clara looking truly relaxed is when she's baking. It's horrible thinking about how much stress I've caused her since I got here.

'I promise I won't let you down again,' I say, looking at the almonds. I wish I really mean it, but I know that I don't. How can I ever not be friends with Holly?

There's a second's silence. Then I hear Aunt Clara putting her bowl down on the table.

'You haven't ever let me down,' she says softly. 'It's just – it's been a big adjustment for both of us, you moving here, that's all.'

I look up at her and smile. She nods at me, then picks up her bowl and carries on mixing.

By the time I leave for school the kitchen is full of trays of quiches and cakes and pies all ready for baking. I'm under strict instructions from Aunt Clara to start putting them in the oven as soon as I get back from school as she has to go and pick the

212

author up from the train station.

I walk to school on my own. When Holly texted me last night to find out what was wrong I told her I'd meet her in the stairwell by our form room to explain. When I get there she's sitting on the bottom step reading. As soon as I see her I feel sad. It's going to be so hard pretending not to be friends with her, and even harder trying to explain why.

'Nessa!' she exclaims, looking up from her book. 'How are you? What happened yesterday? What was wrong with your aunt?'

I sit down next to her. I don't know where to start.

'Is it bad news? You can tell me. Do you have to leave Fairhollow High?'

'Yes and no.'

'What do you mean?' Holly frowns.

I shift awkwardly on the step. 'I don't have to leave – not yet anyway – but . . .'

'What?'

I take a deep breath. 'Aunt Clara says I'm not

allowed to be friends with you.'

'What? But why?' Holly jumps to her feet and stares down at me, her face wrinkled in a frown. 'She says we can't be friends?'

I nod.

'But– but–' The bell rings for registration and the sound of students entering the building comes rumbling down the corridor, stopping Holly mid-sentence.

'I'm not listening to her. We can still be friends here,' I say quickly, 'we just won't be able to see each other outside of school.'

'But outside of school is the best bit of being friends. It's where all the fun stuff happens.' Holly looks around the stairwell in despair. 'This is where we have to do Algebra and Physics. This is where friendships come to die.'

I can't help grinning at this. I get to my feet and take hold of Holly's hand. 'Our friendship is not going to die. We just have to keep it secret for a bit so that Aunt Clara will let me stay at Fairhollow High. OK?'

I feel horrible. I'm letting Aunt Clara down.

Holly sighs. 'OK.'

As I go to give her a hug, the door crashes open and Izzy, Vivien and Stephen stride into the stairwell.

'Ooh, how sweet,' Izzy hisses.

'What are you going to do when your new friend leaves?' Vivien says to Holly. 'How are you going to cope?'

'She's not leaving!' Holly says fiercely.

'Oh yeah?' Stephen snarls.

I step in between him and Holly and stare him right in the eyes. The second I feel his contempt I block it by thinking of the tree. 'Yeah.'

'That's what you think,' he says with an evil grin, but the effect is totally spoilt by his lack of eyebrows.

'We're going to make sure you leave Fairhollow for good and there's nothing you can do to stop us,' Izzy says, the hate radiating off her.

'I wouldn't be so sure about that,' I say, feeling

a sudden surge of strength.

Stephen laughs in my face. 'What can you do?' he sneers.

'Hmm, what can we do?' I tilt my head to one side like I'm thinking. 'Such a shame about your eyebrows. Losing them really has ruined your entire face.'

Stephen stares at me. I feel confusion, then shock, then anger coming off him in waves. Each time I block the feeling my strength grows.

'Amazing what you can do with a Bunsen burner,' Holly chimes up behind me.

I look at Izzy and Vivien. Their mouths are hanging open in shock. 'I'd be really careful in Science from now on if I were you,' I say to them. 'It would be terrible if your hair was to get singed like poor Stephen's eyebrows. Especially when you obviously spend so long trying to get it to look perfect.'

Izzy's face flushes red with anger.

'Come on,' she snaps to the other two and they

start heading up the stairs. Vivien glances nervously behind her as she leaves.

As soon as they've gone, Holly and I look at each other and start to laugh.

'Oh my God, that was epic!' Holly exclaims.

'I know!' I grin at her. 'And the best thing was, the more I blocked their emotions, the stronger I felt.'

Holly nods. 'I could tell. And I think they could too. Did you see Stephen's face?'

'Yes, and Izzy's.'

'And Vivien's. She practically started crying when you said that thing about her hair.' Holly looks at me. 'I think we might have done it: shown them that we're just as strong as they are. Maybe now they'll leave us alone.'

I link arms with her and we start walking up the stairs. I'm still glowing with strength. 'I think you might be right.'

22

For the rest of the day, the feeling that we've got Izzy and the others running scared continues to grow. They don't even look at us let alone try to get us into trouble. Even when I'm partnered with Vivien in Gym I sense a new feeling coming from her – it's like the hatred's been watered down. Watered down with fear.

At the end of the day my report card is full of ticks and glowing comments. The only bad bit is not being able to walk home with Holly.

'I'll email you later,' she says. We've agreed that email is probably the safest way for us to communicate without Aunt Clara finding out.

Once Holly's left I hurry up to the form room to hand my report card in to Mr Matthews. I need to get home quickly to put the food in the oven. As usual, Mr Matthews is sitting behind a teetering pile of marking.

'Ah, Nessa,' he says as I come in. 'Report card time, is it?.'

I nod and pull the card out of my bag.

Mr Matthews looks at it and starts to beam. 'This is wonderful,' he says. 'Very well done. Very well done indeed.' He starts searching around his desk for a pen, even though he's got one tucked behind each ear. Finally he finds one and signs the card. 'Keep up the good work,' he says, handing it back to me and going straight back to his marking.

'Thank you, sir.' I go to leave but the classroom door slams shut. I rattle the handle and pull on it but the door is wedged tight.

'Is everything OK?' Mr Matthews puts his pen down and looks over at me.

'I can't get out. The door's stuck.'

Mr Matthews sighs. 'Oh not again! How many times does this have to happen before the caretaker will take me seriously?'

He gets up from his desk and comes over to join me. But no matter how hard he pulls, the door won't budge.

'Don't worry,' he says brightly. 'I'll call down to reception.' He starts patting his pockets. 'Where's my mobile telephone? Did I bring it today? Oh dear. I don't think I did.' He starts rifling through all papers on his desk. Finally he looks at me apologetically. 'I'm so sorry, I appear to have left it at home. I don't suppose you have a telephone on you?'

I fish my phone out of my bag but it has no bars of signal. 'I don't have any reception,' I say, starting to feel slightly panicked.

Mr Matthews sighs and shakes his head. 'Oh dear.' Then his face brightens. 'Don't worry. There must be someone still about. I'm sure they'll hear us if we call for help.'

In the end it takes us nearly half an hour to be

rescued, with Mr Matthews and me taking it in turns to yell 'help' like we're in a disaster movie, until finally, a cleaner hears us and manages to barge the door open. I leave Mr Matthews huffing and puffing about the caretaker and I race out of school. Aunt Clara will be well on her way to collecting her author now.

As I leave the school gates, my phone finally gets reception back. I try ringing Aunt Clara to let her know I've been held up but there's no reply. I run along the school driveway. I have to get back to get the food cooked. Just as I get to the High Street my phone starts to ring. It's a call from an unknown number – which usually means it's Dad calling from abroad.

'Hello.'

'Oh, Nessa, thank God you answered.'

'Holly! What's wrong?'

'You have to come to your aunt's shop quickly.'

Fear and panic start churning in my stomach. 'What? Why? What are you doing there?'

'Please,' Holly says, 'it's an emergency.'

The line goes dead. I quickly send Holly a text:

Don't worry I'm 5 mins from Paper Soul see you there

I start running even faster.

The cold winter air smells of bonfires. Normally it's a smell I love but now I can't enjoy it all. All I can think is that something must be badly wrong for Holly to have gone to Paper Soul. Maybe something's happened to Aunt Clara. Maybe that's why she didn't answer the phone. I'm running so fast now my legs feel like lead and my lungs are burning. When I get to the shop the only lights on are the ones in the window, highlighting the display for the book launch tonight. My phone chimes with a text. It's from Holly:

What do you mean? Is everything ok? Hxx

I stare at the text for a minute, totally confused. Then I quickly unlock the door and step inside. A strong smell of smoke hits me. But it's not coming from the bonfires outside, it's coming from inside.

'Holly?' I call, rushing towards the café. 'Aunt Clara?' The smell of smoke is getting stronger and stronger. It's coming from the kitchen.

'Aunt Clara,' I shout as I race towards the kitchen door.

'Nessa, you're just in time!'

I freeze as I hear Izzy's voice. It's coming from the kitchen too. Then I open the door and though a haze of smoke, I see Izzy standing next to a worktop holding a rolling pin. She lifts it up and brings it smashing down on to one of the quiches Aunt Clara and I made this morning. Stephen and Vivien are standing either side of her. I take a step towards them.

'What are you doing? How did you get in here?' I look around the kitchen. All the pies we'd laid out ready to cook have been smashed to pieces, and everywhere is covered in a white film of flour.

'Nessa!' I jump at the sound of Holly's voice from out in the shop. 'Nessa? Where are you?'

'In the kitchen,' I yell.

'Oh my God! What's going on?' Holly cries as she enters.

'Well, isn't this the place to be tonight,' Izzy sneers. 'For you two, anyway. I'm afraid we won't be able to stick around, but we're going to have loads of fun imagining what your aunt will say when she sees what you've done to her lovely food.'

'You've set me up,' I stammer, trying to take it all in.

'Yes,' Vivien says with an evil laugh. 'And I'm pretty certain that when your aunt sees all this she's going to send you right back where you came from.'

'I told you we'd make your life hell,' Izzy hisses, taking a step towards me. Her hands are covered in flour and there's a fleck of dough in her hair.

'You're no match for us. You never were.'

I look at her and shake my head. 'You're evil.'

Izzy laughs. 'Thanks. I'll take that as a compliment. But it wasn't just me.' She turns to Vivien. 'Vivien here is an amazing mimic – quite an awesome power, don't you think?'

Vivien throws her head back and laughs, then she turns to me with a look of fake concern on her face. 'Oh, Nessa, thank God you answered,' she says in Holly's voice. 'You have to come to your aunt's shop quickly. Please, it's an emergency.'

I hear Holly gasp behind me.

'And with Stephen able to walk through walls,' Izzy continues, 'getting into this place was a piece of cake. And speaking of cake . . .' she turns and looks at the oven. Smoke is now pouring from the door.

'We put some brownies on for you,' Vivien sniggers. 'Do you think they're ready yet?'

Holly races past me and opens the oven door. Bright orange flames come bursting out and Holly leaps back.

'Are you OK?' I call.

'Yes.' Holly holds her hands out towards the fire. The flames crackle and spit, then die down slightly. 'I can't put it out, but I can stop it from spreading – I think.'

I look around for something to fill with water, but the smoke's so thick now it's hard to see.

'I think it's time we were leaving,' Izzy says. 'Come on, you two.'

'What?' Holly cries. 'You can't leave. The whole shop might burn down. You've got to get help.'

Izzy purses her lips in a smug grin. 'I don't think so.'

A white-hot rage floods my body, and this time it's all mine. I can't believe they'd go this far to get me to leave Fairhollow. I can't believe they're prepared to wreck Aunt Clara's shop.

'Come on, guys,' Izzy says to Vivien and Stephen. She goes to take a step but her legs remain motionless. She tries again, but it's like she's stuck in mud.

'What's happening?' she cries. 'I can't move.'

I feel a tremor of excitement; my powers are working. They're keeping her stuck. I continue staring at Izzy, focusing every thought in my head on her not being able to move.

'I can't walk!' Izzy shrieks, looking terrified now.

Out of the corner of my eye I see Vivien and Stephen exchange worried glances.

'Come on, Iz,' Stephen urges her. 'Stop messing about.'

'I'm not messing!' Izzy yells. 'I can't move my legs!'

I'm really tired from concentrating so hard, but I make myself stay focused. 'Actually, I really think *we* ought to leave,' I say calmly. 'The oven could blow at any minute so it's not safe for us to stay here. What do you think, Holly?' I hold my breath, hoping she'll realise what I'm trying to do.

'Yes,' Holly says. 'Let's go and call the fire brigade.' She looks at Izzy. 'Wow, I bet you guys must really regret pulling this stunt now.'

'But you can't leave us here,' Izzy cries. Her voice is as small as a frightened child's.

'It looks like we're going to have to,' I say calmly, still focusing every ounce of my energy on keeping her still.

'That won't be necessary,' says a voice says from the doorway. 'I think these three have learnt their lesson, don't you?'

'Aunt Clara!' I turn and look at her, feeling light-headed from concentration. Behind me, Izzy starts to whimper.

Aunt Clara marches over to the oven. She's holding a fire extinguisher which she quickly points at the flames, smothering them in white foam. Holly steps back and clasps her hands together, looking as exhausted as I feel.

Izzy, Vivien and Stephen stand huddled together in shock. Aunt Clara turns to look at them, her green eyes glinting with anger. 'I want you three out of here and I don't want you ever coming back. Do you understand?'

They nod meekly, then turn and flee. Aunt Clara runs over to the window and flings it open.

228

As the smoke clears, the devastation in the kitchen looks even worse.

'Um, I know this all looks really bad– but I can explain . . .' I say.

Holly edges over to me. Her face is flushed and streaked with black from the smoke. We look each other helplessly and I know Holly's thinking exactly the same as me. What's Aunt Clara going to say about her being here?

'There's no need to explain,' Aunt Clara says. She comes over and puts her arm round my shoulders. 'I know,' she says quietly. 'I know you're a Silver Witch.' She reaches out and to my surprise she wraps her other arm around Holly's shoulders. 'And I know you are too, Holly.'

'But – how?' I gasp.

Aunt Clara looks down at the floor and sighs. 'Because, as they say, it takes one to know one.'

23

'You're – you're a – Silver Witch?' I stammer, my mind reeling with shock.

Aunt Clara nods. 'And we need to have a serious chat. Let me go and put some signs in the window saying tonight's event's cancelled.'

I clap my hand to my mouth. 'Oh my God! Your launch! Where's the author?' I look over at the kitchen door, half expecting a bewildered writer to be standing there.

'In his bed sick with flu, thank goodness,' Aunt Clara says, looking around at all the mess. 'He got halfway here and had to go home again. I didn't find out until I'd got to the station. Stay here, I'll be back in two ticks.'

Holly and I watch as Aunt Clara hurries off into the shop.

'She's a . . .' Holly whispers, her brown eyes wide.

'Witch,' I finish, shaking my head. I still can't believe this.

We stand there in silence until Aunt Clara gets back.

'Come on, I need to show you girls something,' she says, leading us into the storeroom at the very back of the shop. She heads over to a bookshelf and takes down a huge book.

'Wow, it's even bigger than *The Lord of the Rings*,' Holly whispers in awe as Aunt Clara hands it to her. 'Is it – is it a book of spells?'

'No, it is not,' Aunt Clara mutters. 'It's a book of vegan recipes.' She fiddles around in the empty space left by the book, and suddenly the shelf swings forwards from the wall.

'Oh my God! It's a concealed door!' Holly looks

like she might explode with excitement. 'This is the Best. Thing. Ever.'

Aunt Clara looks at Holly and shakes her head – but thankfully she's smiling. All her dislike of Holly seems to have vanished. 'Come on,' she says, leading us behind the bookshelf and down a steep flight of stone steps.

We come out into a darkened basement. Aunt Clara picks up a box of matches and lights several huge candles dotted about the room. As my eyes adjust to the flickering light, I see that two of the walls are lined with bookshelves. Next to the far wall there's an antique, bureau-style desk and a well-worn sofa draped in a patchwork throw.

'Wow, this place is epic,' Holly whispers. The flames on the candles start bobbing about excitedly.

'That's enough of that, young lady,' Aunt Clara says. 'I think you've done enough energy harnessing for one day, don't you?'

Holly looks sheepish. 'I'm sorry. I'm not very good at controlling it yet.'

Aunt Clara nods. 'Well, you did a very good job of controlling it in the kitchen. It's thanks to you I still *have* a kitchen. And don't worry, I'll help you get that power of yours under control.'

'Thank you!' Holly squeaks in excitement.

We sit down on the sofa and Aunt Clara pulls a battered old trunk over from a corner of the room. It's covered in faded stickers. She opens the trunk and starts rifling through it. Finally, she pulls out a photo and hands it to me. It's of Aunt Clara and Mum sitting under a tree. At first I'm too busy looking at the long capes they're wearing to recognise it. But then I do.

'The old oak tree!' I gasp.

Aunt Clara sits down next to me. 'It's where we used to gather,' she says.

'You and Mum?' I say, not sure what she's trying to say.

'Yes. And the other Silver Witches.'

I stare at her in shock. 'Mum was a witch too?'

Aunt Clara nods and I feel a wave of sadness

coming from her so strong that it makes a lump form in the back of my throat.

'Cool!' Holly says. 'Your mum was a Silver Witch.'

'She *was* . . .' Aunt Clara breaks off, the sorrow I'm picking up from her making my heart ache.

'What is it?' I say, shivering suddenly.

'She – she went over to the other side,' Aunt Clara says, her voice barely more than a whisper.

I look at her blankly. 'What?'

'The Blood Witches.'

Holly gasps.

My skin starts crawling with dread. 'What? Why? Why would she do that?'

Aunt Clara looks down into her lap. 'To save you.'

'Save me from what? I don't understand.' My eyes fill with tears.

'You were so ill as a baby,' Aunt Clara says, 'the doctors told Celeste there was nothing more they could do. One of the Blood Witches in Fairhollow was a very powerful healer. Celeste went to see him, desperate for his help. He agreed but at a very high price.'

I turn so that I'm directly facing Aunt Clara. 'What did he do?'

Aunt Clara's eyes are glassy with tears now too. 'He demanded she switched allegiance and became one of them.'

I shake my head. I can't believe it. I *won't* believe it. 'No way. Not my mum.'

Aunt Clara sniffs and wipes her eyes. 'I'm afraid so. She was a very powerful empath, Nessa – one of the most powerful empaths Fairhollow has ever known. The Blood witches wanted that power for themselves so they could wreak more evil.'

'But Mum – she couldn't be evil, she –'

'She loved you so very much,' Aunt Clara cuts in. 'There was no way she could have let you die.'

I nod, reluctantly. 'So what happened?'

'The healer cured you, and then it was Celeste's turn to deliver her side of the bargain.'

'She – she helped them?'

Aunt Clara nods. I don't even bother trying to block the sorrow coming from her. My own is so strong it wouldn't make any difference. 'Your father was broken-hearted.'

I stare at her in disbelief. 'Dad knew?'

'Yes. He couldn't bear to see what they'd done to her, and he didn't want you exposed to their evil, so he asked her to leave.'

I keep staring at Aunt Clara. 'Dad knew Mum was a witch?'

Aunt Clara nods. 'Yes.'

'But – but he's so anti-everything supernatural. He says it's all a load of mumbo-jumbo.'

Aunt Clara sighs. 'He didn't want you to know anything about it. He was trying to protect you from it all.'

I close my eyes and try to make sense of everything. I think of how Dad has always been so reluctant to talk about Mum and how I'd always put it down to him being too heartbroken. I think of how he always rants about Halloween and how he never let me go trick-or-treating. It wasn't because he thought it was a load of rubbish, it was the opposite. It was because he knew it was true – that witches actually do exist. And then I think of Mum and the few treasured memories I have of her, smiling and sunny and sweet. How could she have become like Izzy and Vivien? It doesn't seem possible.

Aunt Clara takes hold of my hand. 'This is hard for me to say, and I'm sure even harder for you to hear, but your mum quickly found her new life intolerable. She tried to leave but the Blood Witch tie was too strong. She . . . she died in a spell that went wrong.'

We sit in silence for a moment. I'm comforted by the waves of love and concern coming from Aunt Clara and Holly either side of me. Instead of blocking them, I soak them up.

'You're an empath too, aren't you?' Aunt Clara says, finally breaking the silence.

I nod.

'I thought so, from the moment you got here. I sensed it. My powers are faded now, but I could still tell.'

I look at her. 'Are you an empath too?'

Aunt Clara nods. 'It must run in the family. Although I haven't practised for many years. Not since . . . Celeste.' Her face draws into a tight frown. 'After what those witches put her through, I didn't want anything more to do with it, and I wanted to protect you from it too. That's the only reason your dad sent you to stay with me. He knows I turned my back on witchcraft after Celeste died.' Aunt Clara sighs. 'But I guess I was in denial. I thought if I just buried my head in the sand and pretended I hadn't realised you had the gift, then it would somehow go away.' She leans forwards to look at Holly. 'That's why I was so horrible to you, Holly. I do hope you can forgive me, but I knew your grandma. I remember her telling me when you were just a child that she knew you were one of us. When

I heard that Nessa had become friends with you, I panicked. I'm so sorry.'

'Will you really help us?' Holly asks shyly. 'My grandma died before I realised I was a witch and my mum doesn't know anything about it. I have so many questions and I know Nessa does too. Would you tell us some more about what being a witch means?'

'I think I have to,' Aunt Clara replies. 'But first, let me go and get some refreshments. You girls used a lot of power today, you must be exhausted.'

We both nod and smile and Aunt Clara heads up to the kitchen. She returns with a tray containing a pot of ginger tea and a plate of brownies. 'Luckily, I made a batch earlier,' she says with a wry smile. 'The ones our friends baked have turned to charcoal.'

I take a brownie from the plate and take a bite. It's weird, because even though I know it's made from beetroot it tastes delicious to me now – really chocolatey and comforting. I guess my tastebuds have finally become vegan.

'So, what do you girls want to know?' Aunt Clara says, sitting cross-legged on the floor in front of us. The flickering candlelight makes her red hair look like flames.

'Everything!' Holly mumbles through a mouth full of brownie.

'OK,' Aunt Clara says, putting her cup of tea down on the carpet. 'A witch's power starts coming through when they turn thirteen.'

'As if puberty wasn't bad enough,' Holly mutters and we all laugh.

'Their power can be one of nine different things,' Aunt Clara continues. 'They can be an empath, like you and me, Nessa, or an energy harnesser like Holly.'

'And my grandma was a weathercaster,' Holly says.

Aunt Clara nods. 'Yes, she was. And then there are some witches who are telekinetic.'

'Teleki-what-ic?' I say with a frown.

'Telekinetic,' Aunt Clara replies. 'They can move

objects with their mind.'

'Oh, why couldn't I have got that one?' Holly says with a sigh. 'I'd have been able to stay in bed all day and make books float down from the bookshelf.'

'The whole world doesn't revolve around books, you know,' I say, giving her a playful nudge.

'*My* whole world does,' Holly says with a grin. She turns to Aunt Clara. 'So, what other powers are there?'

'Well, a phantom can make themselves invisible.'

'What?' Holly turns to me with wide eyes. 'Seriously, why are the other powers all so much cooler than mine?'

'Can they also travel through walls?' I say, remembering what Izzy said earlier about Stephen and how he let them into the shop.

Aunt Clara nods. 'Yes. It's a very tricky power if it gets into the wrong hands.'

'Tell me about it,' I mutter. That must have been how Stephen found out about me moving schools. He must have walked into Mr Bailey's office.

'And a healer can obviously heal people and animals and plants,' Aunt Clara says, 'and an alchemist creates medicines.' She frowns. 'Or poisons. Then there's the mimic, who's able to do impressions of other people.'

'Vivien,' Holly and I say in unison.

Aunt Clara looks at us. 'One of the girls who was here before?'

I nod. 'Yes, the one with the dark hair.'

'Oh dear. Well, you'll need to be very careful around her. The mimic starts by doing impressions of voices but as their power develops they're able to look like other people too.'

'No way!' Holly looks at me shocked. 'And finally,' Aunt Clara says, 'there's the time-shifter.'

'What does that one do?' Holly asks.

'They're able to slow time,' Aunt Clara says. 'Sometimes they can even stop it and in some very rare cases, a time-shifter is able to reverse time.'

'Cool,' Holly whispers.

But I'm filled with dread. Is Izzy a time-shifter?

It would explain how she managed to wreak so much damage in the shop before I got home.

'Are you OK?' Aunt Clara says, looking at me.

'Yes – I – are you picking up my feelings?'

She nods and gives an embarrassed grin. 'As I said, my powers are fading now – the older generation of witches start to lose their powers as soon as the new generation gain theirs, but I can still tell when someone's having a strong emotion. What's wrong?'

'I think Izzy might be a time-shifter.'

We sit in silence for a moment.

Aunt Clara shakes her head. 'So the Blood Witches have a time-shifter and a mimic in this generation.' She sighs, and worry ripples from her in dark waves.

'Are witches born Blood or Silver?' Holly asks.

Aunt Clara shakes her head. 'No, each witch has to choose which side they want to be on.'

'But why are there different sides in the first place?' I ask.

'Well, it wasn't always that way,' Aunt Clara says. 'Hundreds of years ago witches lived together in harmony in Fairhollow, only using their powers for the good of the community. But in the 1400s, twin witches were born, Gregor and Elizabeth. Elizabeth wanted to use her power as an empath for her own good, by manipulating people and controlling them, but Gregor wouldn't agree and so they split.'

'Into the Blood and Silver Witches?' I say.

'Yes.'

My heart sinks as I realise the implications of this. 'So does that mean we have to spend the rest of our lives battling Izzy and the others?'

'I think I'd rather be a lawyer,' Holly mutters.

'No. Not necessarily,' Aunt Clara replies. 'If you manage to complete your pente before them they'll lose their powers.'

Holly frowns. 'What's a pente?'

'A group of five witches.' Aunt Clara sits up straight. 'Whichever side forms a pente first gains supremacy and the other side lose their powers for that generation.'

'So, if we find three other Silver Witches, Izzy and the others will lose their power?' I ask, feeling a glimmer of hope.

Aunt Clara nods. 'Yes.'

'But they already have one more witch than us,' Holly says.

'It doesn't matter. They still don't have five.' Aunt Clara leans towards us, looking deadly serious. 'It's vital that you complete your pente first. What they did here today was nothing compared to what will happen if they gain supremacy.'

A shiver of dread runs up my spine. 'What do you mean?'

'Of course, it might not matter,' Aunt Clara picks up her tea and takes a sip. 'There might not be any more witches in Fairhollow in your generation. And if there are, they might not want to join the Blood Witches.'

'And then what happens?' Holly asks.

'Well, if they can't form a pente before they turn sixteen, they'll never get supremacy. That's what happened in my generation. The Blood Witches haven't had supremacy for a long time now. But it means this new generation will be itching to gain power. You girls will have to be on your guard, and you'll have to try and find some more Silver Witches.'

Holly lets out a huge yawn, which immediately sets me off.

'I think the best thing you girls can do right now is get a good night's sleep,' Aunt Clara says, standing up. 'Using so much power will have drained you. Holly, why don't you stay here tonight? I'm sure Nessa would be glad of your company.'

I nod and smile gratefully.

'What? Like a sleepover?' Holly says excitedly.

Aunt Clara laughs and nods. 'Yes, like a sleepover.'

While Holly texts Svetlana to let her know, I follow Aunt Clara up into the kitchen. With all of the spilt flour and fire extinguisher foam, it looks as if there's been some kind of freak indoor snowstorm.

'Don't you want a hand tidying this up?' I say.

Aunt Clara shakes her head. 'I'll be fine.'

'But it'll take ages.'

She looks at me and smiles. 'Good job I only need four hours' sleep.'

I smile back at her. An invisible cord of love and warmth connects us.

'Go on,' she says with a smile. 'Get on up to bed.'

24

Even though Aunt Clara's revelations were earth-shattering, and even though I'm massively excited at the prospect of Holly being allowed for a sleepover, I'm so tired I fall asleep pretty much the second my head hits the pillow. When I wake the next morning the revelations of the night before come charging back into my head in a crazy rush. My mum was a witch. Aunt Clara's a witch! And my dad knows! Even though I'm really sad about what happened to my mum, I feel determined too. She went through all of that so that I could live. I owe it to her not to let the Blood Witches gain supremacy. I owe it to her to use my powers for good.

'Ness, are you awake?'

I roll on to my side and look down through the darkness at the outline of Holly, lying on the air bed. 'Yes. How did you sleep?'

'Great, you know, considering all the stuff that happened last night.'

'Me too.'

'It's so cool that your aunt's a witch.'

'I know. I never would have guessed!' I lean over and turn on my bedside lamp.

Holly sits up, her curly hair all flat on one side from where she's been sleeping. 'I'm so glad we've got someone to help us and teach us about our powers.'

I nod.

Holly sighs. 'The trouble is, I now have about a million more questions I want to ask.'

I laugh. 'Me too. Shall we go and see if she's up yet?'

Holly's out of bed before I even finish the question.

We trudge into the kitchen in our pyjamas.

'Wowsers!' Holly exclaims as we look around the room.

It's like the fire never happened. Every surface is sparkling and there's the delicious smell of freshly-baking bread coming from the oven. Aunt Clara is sat at the table sipping a mug of tea, immaculately dressed and made-up like she's been awake for hours.

'Did you do all this by yourself?' Holly says.

Aunt Clara nods.

'It looks amazing, doesn't it Nessa?' Holly looks at me but I can't reply. I can't say anything. I can't tear my eyes from the table. The letter about my school transfer is lying open right in front of Aunt Clara, like she's about to sign it. I feel sick with disappointment. After what happened yesterday Aunt Clara probably wants me as far away as possible from Izzy and the others. I can't really blame her. But how can I leave Holly to face them on her own?

'Don't fret, Nessa,' Aunt Clara says gently. Then she looks at Holly and smiles. 'Holly, would you please do the honours – gently, mind!'

Holly looks at her blankly for a second, then

a massive grin spreads across her face. 'Cool!' she exclaims, before looking at the letter and crinkling up her nose. The letter starts glowing red at the edges. Then it starts to curl. Holly keeps on staring at it until the entire letter has disintegrated into a pile of ashes.

Aunt Clara claps. 'Good work! Nicely controlled!'

'Thank you.' Holly grins. 'I got your message telling me to burn it in my head. It was so cool, like you sent me a psychic text.' She turns to me and grins. 'Seriously, Nessa, your power is the best. Just think, when you're able to do that, you won't even need a phone!'

I laugh, still trying to make sense of what just happened. Aunt Clara comes over and takes hold of my hand. 'There's no way I'm separating you two,' she says. 'Not now I've seen how dangerous these new Blood Witches are. I want to teach you both about witchcraft so that you're strong enough to stand up to them. That's if you want me to . . . ?'

'Of course I want you to,' I say, squeezing Aunt Clara's hand. 'We've got to complete the pente and stop the Blood Witches for once and for all – for our generation at least. Right, Holly?'

Holly nods, her eyes gleaming with excitement.

Aunt Clara smiles at us, then she steps forwards and puts her hand on the table. She gestures at us to do the same, with our fingertips touching.

'Silver me, Silver you,' she says softly, 'Silver us, Silver true.' Then she nods at us to join in.

My skin tingles as we start reciting the words. 'Silver me, Silver you, Silver us, Silver true.'

The tingling feeling grows. I feel it passing up through my body, out of my fingers and into the others, then coming back from them into me.

'Silver me, Silver you, Silver us, Silver true.'

As I look at Holly and Aunt Clara and we continue to chant the words I'm filled with happiness and hope. It's like I've just found something I didn't even know I was looking for. It's like I'm finally where I belong.

What's next for Nessa
at Fairhollow High?

And who has something to hide?

Find out in . . .

THE

WITCHES

OF

FAIRHOLLOW HIGH

The
SECRET

Coming Feb 2017